Don't turn off the Lights Tonight

Ishita Banik

Ukiyoto Publishing

Acknowledgements

A big thanks to everyone- who stood by me throughout this journey, my closest family, friends, and most importantly, my grandmother, hearing whose stories I grew up.

Thanks to my amazing publishing team for their hard work, without whom my stories would have been just an unfulfilled dream.

Lastly, thanks to my readers, for always supporting me and picking up my book once again! Cheers!

Contents

Her eyes were dark blue.
The same got her brother,
but only after her death.

The Mirage of the Night

Since the time they moved in the new house, Nia had been complaining about something strange. Nehal had tried many times to make her understand, she even stopped reading stories to her, but she wouldn't stop blabbering.

'It's quite normal. New place and all…you know? you don't need to worry. I will come soon,' Nikhil told over the call. Nehal was doing her household chores and her eyes were on the ceiling, automatically. They were in the fourth floor and the fifth floor was fully closed. To be honest, she often got worried hearing Nia's complaints. She had never done that before. And there was still one week left for Nikhil to arrive. 'Yes, I understand. No problem.' Nehal was feeling restless inside, but didn't tell him anything. Let him take his own time, she thought. After hanging up, Nehal went to the terrace to put clothes for drying. There was no one on the terrace. And she noticed the entire fifth floor was closed and deserted. Sometimes the silence creeped her out. She was not habituated to staying in such an aloof place. But their apartment was more than luxurious and from the next month Nikhil would start going to his new office too, so they were supposed to settle down at least for the next 5 years.

'Mummy, I have seen him again!' Nia pointed her fingers towards the ceiling. Nehal was alert this time, there are certain tones of children, which convey that they are not lying. And Nia's tone was like that.

'No prank Nia! Come! It's lunchtime!' Nehal walked towards the kitchen while observing the white ceiling and the attached glossy fan.

'I am not lying mummy! He was looking at me and he won't speak…ever!' she complained, somehow her eyes told she was not lying.

'Where has he gone then?!' Nehal was feeling uncomfortable, she was feeling the light drops of sweat near the bangs of her hair on her forehead.

Nia didn't reply but kept staring at the ceiling. 'Nia, finish your food. Mumma has work to finish. Be a good girl, okay?' Nehal carried her to place her on the chair in front of their dining table, Nia's eyes were glued to the ceiling. In the next moment, something unexpected happened. Nehal was approaching the switchboard while wiping her forehead with her dupatta, Nia was just about to say something; Nehal turned on the fan by that time and at the very moment, there was a glass-cracking scream along with Nia's fine screaming voice. Nehal, with both her hands in her ears, watched a black bird flying out of her window. She rushed to Nia, 'Why did you shout?' She hugged her, still trying to figure out the loud screaming, it was definitely not of any bird.

'Mummy…the man…he was there… sitting on the fan, I tried to stop you!'

'What are you saying?' Nehal was more scared than ever, her heart was beating loudly in her ears. For the first time, she thought, she believed Nia, even without seeing what Nia saw.

'That was just a bird, Nia. Why do you keep saying that?' Nehal looked into her eyes, and there was fear in her doe-like innocent eyes. *Why those eyes will be scared if she is making it up?'* Nehal thought.

'Bird? You almost cut one of its wings, mummy. He jumped out of the window!' She pointed her finger towards the open window, through which the bird just flew out. Nia was slightly shaking while she spoke.

'Okay. Let me see?' Nehal went near the window and looked around through it. She was not expecting any man anyway, it was just to comfort Nia.

'Nia! There is no man!' she shouted making her voice as normal as possible. But there was still disbelief in Nia's eyes.

'Okay, come see!'

Nia came by her side, looking around while pasting herself near her mother's waist. 'If someone was here, he must have left. He must be some thief Nia. Now I am closing all the doors and windows, he can't come again, okay? And if you see him near our home, tell me, I will call the police!'

Nia looked assured this time. Nehal closed all the windows and doors and then fed her lunch. Both looked relaxed and comfortable, while one was just acting to assure the other.

'The number you are trying to call is not reachable.' Again the same thing and Nehal was getting impatient. She was calling Nikhil's mother. It was strange to call her for the first time, but it was urgent. Surprisingly, it said the same thing, her number was not reachable. It was almost night, and she couldn't call his office to convey anything.

'Call me when you get this. Need to tell you about something happening here,' Nehal typed the text message, then backspaced it and typed again, *'Called you. Your number is not reachable. We are good. Love you,'* she hit the send button and went to sleep hugging Nia near her chest.

That night Nehal saw a very weird dream. She saw that she was standing alone in a desert, walking endlessly. She was calling Nia and Nikhil by their names, but there was no one. Then she saw a big black bird chasing her and she was running breathlessly. Finally, she found Nikhil standing far away and calling her name, the sound was fading in and out in the blowing wind. She ran towards him and almost collided against his chest, trying to catch her breath. She was asking him where Nia was, but Nikhil pushed her away and the big bird jumped on him, the bird was even bigger than she thought, and it didn't fully look like a bird except the wings. She heard Nikhil screaming but she was unable to move even an inch.

'Mummy! Wake up!'

Nehal woke up, sweating and panting profusely. There was burning sunlight outside and the air inside the room felt hot on her cheeks and hands like she was still in that desert. Nia stood up on the bed to switch on the fan and then she handed her mom a glass of water from the bedside table. Nehal finished it in one go and hugged Nia tightly while hearing her own heartbeats. She used to get this sleep paralysis thing sometimes and Nia knew what to do. The rest of the day Nehal kept trying to reach Nikhil several times, but Nikhil's phone was switched off. She even called his office. But the line was busy the entire time. Finally, her mobile rang while she was having dinner with Nia on her lap. There was some connection problem, so their TV was off and it was more silent than usual. The windows were closed and both the mother and daughter were looking at the dark outside the window occasionally. And then her mobile rang. Nehal heart almost skipped a beat, it was such a relief seeing Nikhil's number flashing on her mobile. She gestured Nia to eat and picked up the call. 'Honey, so sorry, I dropped my phone at the office yesterday. There was too much work pressure the whole day. I am coming back tomorrow!' he spoke from the other end.

'Oh! I was so worried...'

'Why? What happened?'

'I called your mother and your office too,' Nehal hesitated. He might not like her calling his mother, but she had no other option.

'Did she speak?' Nikhil asked after a while. He sounded busy doing something.

'No.'

'Okay, no problem. I will see you tomorrow. Love you. Take care.' He hung up shortly after.

Finally, Nehal was feeling so relieved that she totally forgot something unusual she felt while talking. Though she couldn't put a finger on it instantly. She felt some kind of unknown discomfort bubbling inside her, also, she was feeling a déjà vu the entire time. Hanging up the call she took Nia to bed, while herself going through some recent magazines. Suddenly something struck her. In the next moment, she was searching through her phone messages, older chats...after an hour of exhausting search, she found a number and called. 'Hi, hotel Raylakes Inn?'

'Yes, ma'am. How can I help you?'

'Can you give the call to Mr. Nikhil Verma? He is staying in room no. 304.'

'Just a minute ma'am.' The girl on the other side was taking her time while Nehal was waiting silently.

'Ma'am are you there?' the girl asked after a few minutes. 'There is no Nikhil Verma staying in our hotel. Not only in 304, but in no other rooms.'

Nehal again said his full name, company name, and even described him, but the girl at the reception repeated the same thing.

After ending the call, Nehal texted Nikhil, *'Oh, I forgot to ask the hotel name you are staying in. I know you are coming back soon, but can you tell me the name please? You know, sometimes, like yesterday, I get so stressed, so. It's fine if you are sleeping.'* Once she hit the send button, she started scrolling through their chat again…the messages exchanged for the last three months. It all happened so fast and it was beautiful starting from their first meeting to getting married. Most importantly, he got along with Nia so well. In those three months, she forgot the last 5 years of her tormenting marriage. She wanted to live her life freely without depending on anyone after the divorce. But then Nikhil happened to her. It was all too beautiful to resist for her, who was all broken and damaged inside. Nehal heard a beep sound of an incoming message. As she tapped on it, the same hotel name and address floated in front of her eyes. But why did Nikhil lie to her? She heard some sound…like some big bird flapping its wings. Nehal got up and came near the window, from where the sound was coming. Nia was already awake on her bed, looking in the same direction as Nehal. There was only condensed dark outside, while the sound of a fluttering was getting louder. Nia seemed fully absorbed by what she was seeing, her eyes were wide open and unblinkingly staring as if piercing the pitch dark outside. Nehal put her nose on the thick glass of the windowpane as her eyes kept searching for the source of the sound in the dark outside, she could sense some vague movement of wings like some bird was trapped somewhere and trying to get out. The moonless dark sky seemed to make the outside isolated from the rest of the world, where anything could happen at any time. It was like the silent whispers were absorbed in the thin air and in the next moment there was a loud thud with a piercing pain in her left eye, like thousands of needles were pierced there, with a hot foaming fluid flowing between her fingers pressed on her eye. Her right eye saw everything blurred in front of her and by the time she gained her vision back from beneath the teary blurred screen, the pin-drop silence was back in the room. The window in front of her was broken and she stepped over a piece of glass while looking for Nia inside the room. Her left eye felt numb like someone took it out from the socket leaving there only screeching pain to feel. Nia couldn't be found anywhere, nor the sound of the wings could be heard. Only a few black feathers were on the bed and floor of the room. Before she could dial the emergency number with her freezing hands, Nehal saw the Full Moon glowing in the sky- it looked blood-red through her eyes or maybe it really was.

After two days

Srijita tried hard to join the dots, but it didn't make any sense to her. Finally, she was speaking while looking at the pale face of Nehal, who hadn't gained any consciousness since the day Nia and Nikhil went missing, 'Your last few calls were to Nikhil and a hotel. Maybe to connect with him? If I go by the texts and calls made from your mobile, Nikhil and Nia…both got disappeared from the same day. I have only heard about Nikhil from you, never saw him. But you know what's the most puzzling part is?' Srijita looked around, it was early in the morning, and almost no other visitors were there at that time. 'The number you saved as Nikhil in your mobile, got tracked, it was taken in the name of your ex-husband Prithwi, he disappeared since you two got separated…and no one has seen him since that time.' Srijita stopped looking at her face. There were still 24 hours left for her to gain back consciousness, she thought. She noticed a big black bird fluttering its wings near the window, its size was at least twice or thrice of a crow, she had never seen such a big bird here before, it was trying to enter inside. Srijita put on her glasses as she stood up, but the bird was gone already.

Nehal on the other side was slipping into deeper sleep where she hadn't been for years since her childhood. She was in the same desert as she dreamt of a few days ago and everything was happening at a slow pace. This time Nia was with her and she could finally recognize the face of the man…but this time she was utterly confused. She couldn't decide whose face was that-Nikhil or Prithwi. There were big black wings covering the sky and she couldn't see him anymore, she only felt Nia being pulled away from her, she put all her strength to fight back.

Srijita noticed some movement in her left hand like she was trying to wake up. She rushed to call the doctor instantly.

On the other side, the fight was getting intense, the fight was between two unequal forces. Nehal was not coming back without Nia. She was slipping into dense sleep, to an infinite depth at the corner of some other universe, where the difference between eternal sleep was getting blurred. She was surrendering her consciousness into the black holes etched in the endless universe. Her fist was getting tighter, the doctors came to check her vitals, observed her movements, but technically she was losing it. A black feather was on the ground, near the feet of her bed, which fell as her fist loosened slowly. She was fighting the endless inhuman fight, which started from the desert and ended at the eighth floor flat of Mumbai Andheri, a lifeless body was taken away from there before three months, but the remaining intangible part stayed within the same four walls where the five-year-old tormenting marriage ended. While one started fresh or got the illusion of so, the other rotted in the same place in a loop. One story ended, and another began, only to come to a dead-end once again.

The Unfinished Scream

1

"Wow! That's better!" Yashvi thinks as she saves the new manuscript with the name 'FinalBook3'.

She saves the previous draft with the name 'CancelledBook3' and shuts down her laptop. The tired face with dark circles staring through the black screen in front of her finally looks happy!

'It's done! Meeting you tomorrow at 9:30' she drops the text to her editor as she jumps inside the blanket on her bed. It was a very hectic week and she barely got a chance to rest. Diksha is not home yet. She calls her but she doesn't receive. Yashvi drops her a text saying she will be asleep, she can just get in with her keys. She needs a peaceful sleep today!

2

Yashvi hears some unclear sound almost like whispers near her ears…she reaches for Diksha beside her in her sleep and squeezes her hand lightly, "Got a nightmare again?" she asks in a sleepy voice.

"Hmm."

"Ohh…sleep..." she pats her gently while falling back deep in her sleep again.

Next Morning

"Hey! You fine?" Yashvi asks as she takes the elevator, eyes glued to the mobile selecting the book cover.

"Yup all right! So…when are you throwing a party for the big news?" Diksha asks with her excited smile. "You are yet to tell me more about it!"

"Uhh…soon I will if it really manages to be a best-seller again!" Yashvi says mockingly. "And I am gonna tell you the rest at dinner!"

Both of them rush towards their own ways after getting off the elevator as they say bye to each other smiling.

Despite being roommates for more than a year, they have very little time to sit and talk as both are workaholics and not much interested in each other. Apart from being so excited about her stories and books, Diksha has a well-maintained boundary that Yashvi never crossed to become her friend from a roommate. They both have quite good own lives and somehow they were not meant to be friends!

Yashvi gets in the cab as she waits for her designer to respond with the updated book cover. He is one of the most flexible persons to work with in their team, and he is working hard to bring out the best in her book cover this time too!

She hears a faint sound of someone sighing beside her and turns around for the first time leaving her mobile to face a teenage girl with a round, cute face wearing a green color full sleeve top and holding a blue file in her hand. For a few seconds, she gets a déjà vu and in the next moment her mobile rings. The name 'Editor Samriddhi' is flashing on the screen.

"Hey! I got some urgent work at home, can we meet in that café on Bakers Road?" she speaks as soon as Yashvi picks up the call.

"Yup sure! I'll be there!" she says. "Just drop me near BakeFeast Café!" Yashvi says the driver quickly.

-"Cool! See you soon!"

Yashvi collects her bag and pays the driver as the cab pulls over in front of the café in the next few minutes.

3

"So, all set?" Diksha asks taking a spoonful of rice in her mouth. Her eyes look curious as always.

"Yup! Finally!" Yashvi answers joyfully. "And if all goes as planned, we can launch it by next month!" she says happily chewing her food. "Finally, I gave in to what the editor told and it actually turned out to be better you know!" she says sipping water, raising her brows.

"Wow! That's great…but I liked the characters Jay and Ravi so much. You could have kept them!" Diksha says in a tone of complaint and Yashvi likes it when people get so close to the characters that they just refuse to let them go. And Diksha only read a few pages from her previous draft!

"I know!" a smile plays on her face. "But what's coming is even better than what's gone!" she says in a mysterious tone as she gets up from the dinner table taking the empty plates and bowls in her hand.

-"Of course it is!" Diksha looks curious. "Can you say more of it?"

"Well! I think you will prefer to read it more!" Yashvi says with a wink as she walks towards the kitchen.

"What happened?" Diksha asks looking at the dull and tensed face of Yashvi searching for something.

"All are finished," Yashvi says with a blank stare at her laptop screen, her eyes and hands are searching for something restlessly. "I can't find it…it's nowhere!" she says scratching her hair.

-"What?" Diksha comes near her to have a look at her laptop. "What you can't find?"

"The manuscript!" she says in a tensed voice while tapping the keypad and searching her folders restlessly. "Neither my editor can…how can this be possible!"

"You have searched properly? You didn't rename it later or something na?" she sits beside her.

"No I didn't…" she opens a doc file named 'FinalBook3'. "But how can this even be possible?!" she murmurs. "This is not the edited and final manuscript but the draft which I cancelled! I saved the cancelled draft with the name 'cancelledBook3'…I am so sure and this can't be true!" her voice sounds desperate. "I can't find it anywhere…it has just vanished," her eyes are glued to the laptop screen. "Seven new chapters I added there discarding the old ones…" Yashvi murmurs again. "I need to rewrite them all!"

Diksha can't understand what to say…she keeps looking at her panic-stricken face.

4

"What happened? Didn't sleep?" Diksha asks seeing Yashvi sitting up.

"Can't sleep. All my hard work has gone in vain," she says looking at the darkness scattered throughout the room. "All my sleepless nights, endless research and editing…I have to do it all again…from scratch," she says looking at the windowpane barely lit with the dim light of the midnight.

"But what if this was for good only?" Diksha's voice comes floating from the other side of the bed. "In the last draft, which you discarded, so many characters were there…Jay, Ravi, Sheetal…you created them with so much time and devotion."

"So?" Yashvi cuts her off in the midway. "What does that have to do with this?"

"They need their destinies— good or bad," Diksha's voice floats to her like a strong and sharp whisper. "Every creation must have a proper destiny…that's the law of nature. You create them with so much dedication, you bring them to life and then leave them midway…where they will go now? Can't you hear their silent, unfinished scream? You just can't just leave them for nothing! They must end like any other creation, Yashvi. Every creation is bound to end…every start has its own destiny to end…" her voice gets stronger with each passing second. "Give them a destiny or they will get stuck at doing what you left them to do…and that's unnatural."

"Doesn't make any sense," Yashvi mutters with irritation in her voice. "Sleep Diksha, you must be having another nightmare today."

Yashvi rolls back to her side with her head full of thoughts. She keeps looking at the dark blank wall in front of her while thinking how to restart the work from tomorrow again…slowly sleep takes over her.

5

Yashvi hangs up the call after getting confirmed for the hundredth time that her final polished manuscript is actually gone! And surprisingly no one can find it! She reschedules the meeting with her publishing team in the second half. She got up late today morning and it got even later after having that weird conversation with Diksha. She was calling her to wake her up when Diksha said that she just returned in the morning and was super tired. It was true indeed as she was still wearing that glittery short black dress with her face full of make-up. She dragged her up from sleep to ask about yesterday night only to discover that Diksha left for a night out after dinner and Yashvi was fast asleep then. She stayed at her friend's place the whole night and returned at 8 in the morning. She didn't even lay down in her bed yesterday night.

The whole thing just can't be a dream…or, was it? It seemed too real that Yashvi couldn't get convinced fully.

6

Yashvi turns around with the sound of shutting of a car door and her heart skips a beat as she starts getting that unsettling déjà vu again seeing the same girl in her cab- she is wearing the same green top and the same blue cover file is kept on her lap, her sleek fair fingers are tapping on that blue file continuously. As Yashvi looks into her eyes, she manages a casual smile on her tensed face adjusting the hair behind her ear.

It takes a few seconds for Yashvi to remember her own written lines from the discarded manuscript-

'Sheetal took a cab hurriedly and placed herself inside amidst all the terrifying thoughts. Her green long top was touching her knees, her long and sleek fair fingers were tapping restlessly on the blue cover file kept on her lap. All the uncertain thoughts were reminding her of what her nearby future could have in store for her…she looked at the stranger sitting beside her and managed a faint smile on her tensed face while adjusting her hair…'

Yashvi cannot process anything further, she can only hear yesterday night's whisper, "Give them a destiny or they will get stuck at doing what you left them to do…and that's unnatural."

Her mind and body start freezing as she recalls the next few lines of her abandoned first manuscript, the lines which describe how Sheetal got murdered along with the cab driver and another passenger by Jay and Ravi…

Where the Dreams Go?

1

Aaden tries to adjust his eyes to the scorching sunlight falling on his face mercilessly. He calls someone to close the windows and then sits up on his bed in the next few minutes as no one turns up. He rubs his eyes recalling every bit of his dream. The dream was good, there were two/three more girls and boys of his age with whom he was talking his heart out. They were laughing and roaming in the large school building which resembled his present school. The only difference was there were his friends giving him a good time in his dream. He saw themselves emerging out from the school building as the last bell rang and there his parents were waiting for him, they were looking so happy and smiling seeing their son cheerful. He was about to introduce his friends to them, but at that very moment, the dream ended…he woke up.

He gets off the bed with a dark face. The beginning of spring has poured all its aura, sunshine and beauty around their house and in the surrounding garden. Their driver is washing the car with the sprinkling water carrying the droplets from the sunrays, he can hear the light sound of talking and chattering from the kitchen.

"Aadi! Why are you so late!" his mom emerges out from the kitchen with plates in her hands. "Go, take bath fast! I am making your breakfast!"

He nods and walks towards the bathroom attached to his room. While taking bath he finds a few marks of sketch pen on his left arm. He remembers playing with his new friends in his dream. A smile plays on his lips.

2

Nia observes the small room attached to the terrace. It looks the same as it was 20 years ago. She can't believe so many years have passed! She was only eight years old playing around all the places and this used to be her favourite place. She inhales the same mixed fragrance of the old iron, dust and carbon monoxide…it feels like fresh air to her. A lot of memories start rushing back in a blink. Time flies! Really! The whole terrace used to be her biggest playground once, there she used to run around the whole afternoon while taking the bites of fruits from the hands of her grandmother and mother. Every day her grandmother used to tell her a story and she used to imagine it all with her big, curious eyes. There used to be aeroplanes flying over them making the trails of white clouds on the sky and she used to run following it until the aeroplane used to vanish deep inside the blue of the sky. So many people, so much laughter and moments…only memories are there in the big empty house now. She stands near the railing of the terrace, the roads and houses haven't changed that much apart from a few houses which have been rebuilt. She can't recognize most of the faces she has seen till now. She feels a sudden emptiness in her…longing for that one afternoon with all her family members.

She wraps the dupatta around her looking at the setting sun far behind the tall buildings, then she walks slowly inside. She looks at the terrace one last time before locking the doors. The house will be sold finally, but what about the memories? Can those be sold too? She wondered as tears started springing into her eyes.

3

She again hears the knock on the door. She can hear the sound of shoes, plastics and blabbering from outside her door. She hardly slept for an hour or so. It's still dark outside. She gets up with her sleepy eyes and opens the door, there is no one. She again hears the mixed sound of faint talking and giggling from inside. As she passes through the passageway from her room towards the other end of the house, she finds the door of the other flat is locked, she remembers that she locked the entire house and rooms apart from the one she slept in. She feels she is half-asleep and dreaming. She comes back near her room but finds it locked from inside. She tries to unlock it several times but it seems to be locked from inside. All her stuff and mobile too is locked in that room. She takes a few minutes and then rushes downstairs and when she reaches the ground floor, her heart almost stops, the whole floor is full of all the scattered things like someone has thrown out all the things in extreme anger. There are dresses, bangles, toys, sarees, food packets, flower vases, water bottles, pieces of glass and what not like the whole house got stirred up. Nia takes a few steps cautiously as she walks towards the long hallway on the ground floor approaching the other end of the house…all the doors are open, all the windows are inundated with the dim street lights, the spring breeze is swaying the curtains stuck at the windows. The whole house is too silent that it itself sounds like an invisible scream.

She was about to stumble upon something on the floor, but she braces the wall trying hard to not fall on the floor which is a mess now. As she looks down to find what's blocking her way…her body freezes in a moment. She feels the blood rushing through her veins with all the momentum and her eyes get still and stuck at her own cold and lifeless eyes staring back at her.

Three days later

Nia wakes up with a jolt, her whole body is shaking, her eyes get stuck at the ceiling, her hands feel paralyzed, she can't move an inch…sticking to the bed while sweating profusely her mouth struggles to get air, her throat feels choked and dry gasping for air. She can feel her whole room, the light air spreading from the ceiling fan, the floating feathers of the dream-catcher, the tingling silvery sound of the wind chimes…she starts feeling lifeless and numb. She feels death nearby with no escape…

Next morning

Nia drags the chair nearby, her eyes glued to the laptop screen, she keeps scrolling and reading each word and finally, it comes to a halt with the last line of the article-

'Our dreams are not just our imagination. They are intangible entities existing in some other dimensions.'

The whole article has shaken her up a lot as there are a lot of supporting links like the news, press release, scientific research articles and more. She notes down the address and contact number quickly. Instantly she calls the number without waiting any further. After a full ring, the call gets disconnected. She again calls the number as she paces around restlessly in her bedroom. Her whole room is messy, the plates of breakfast are still there on her table, the wet towel is left on her bed. She needs to meet with this person anyhow, as she seems to be the only one whose thoughts match with what she has been experiencing.

"Hello!" a girl speaks from the other side.

"Hey!" Nia swallows as she speaks. "I need an appointment with Dr. Sumedha Paul, today. Is it possible? It's urgent."

"Sure! Your name please?"

"It's Nia. Only Nia," she utters, waiting restlessly for the response.

"All right. Come down at 4:30 pm," she speaks fast. "And be on time, please. She is seeing a lot of people these days."

"Sure! I will…"

The call disconnects abruptly.

4

It's sharp 4:00 pm when she reaches the place. Nia pays the cab driver as she takes quick steps towards the old and big two-storey building in front of her. The address was precise and it took her more than one hour to reach here. She calls the number once but it's engaged.

The place is in Navi Mumbai near one of the oldest apartments of this area. She remembers that she came here once to meet her college friend. Despite being near the main street, there are not many people there. She has the address written clearly, and she knows where to go. It's on the first floor, room no. 21E. That's a strange kind of address, she thinks. The security guard checks her name and appointment time and lets her enter after confirming via intercom.

There are a few people going here and there inside the building. The ground floor looks like a private office, though she didn't notice any signboard while entering. She starts climbing the stairs with the dusty mosaic printed over there and with each step taken forward she finds the place familiar, like she has had many memories over there, and still she can't remember a single one.

She finds the only closed white door on the first floor written 'Dr. Sumedha Paul, Oneirologist'.

-"Your name please?" someone calls her from behind.

"Hey!" Nia turns around to say her name and in the next moment, she gets utterly surprised seeing her old college friend Dishani standing right in front of her. "Disha! You…how are you?"

"Oh! What a surprise!" Dishani smiles joyfully. "I am working here as a receptionist," she says looking down at her writing pad. "Hey…it's your turn I think…just be back…I will be right here!" she says as she opens the door in front of her to let her in. Nia nods, smiling and enters inside.

After almost one hour of discussion, she leaves her chamber. She can't see Dishani anywhere. As she climbs down the empty stairs soaked in the evening haze she starts remembering all her lost memories over there— her tuitions before the board exams, how she fell from the stairs repeatedly since her childhood, different dreams in the same place…different time…mixing up in the same dimension.

"Nia," a soft, light voice speaks from beside her. "Whom did you just meet, you think?"

"Dishani…my old college friend." She looks back, only to find the unfathomable depth of the darkness surrounding her. There are no stairs she was walking on, there is only darkness and nothingness.

"Whom else did you meet here before Nia? Can you remember?"

"My old college friend." Nia can't see anything around her. "I can't remember the name. Where am I? And what's going on? Can you please tell me?"

"Can you remember the face of your old college friend Nia?" the soft voice beneath the dark speaks so lightly that it sounds like a hiss of a snake.

-"Yes…she…"

"Does she look like Dishani?"

"Yes she does," Nia remembers. "Yup I remember, she was Dishani…"

"And what about the other ones Nia? Who are they?"

"My known ones…I don't know…"

"That's what no one knows Nia," the sound of the hissing voice is coiling like a thin snake slowly sliding through her ears. "Where do they go, Nia? Where do your dreams go? Whom you see in your dreams…they are living here Nia…the time, the place, the people…they belong to you…they will keep coming to you …"

Nia feels the temperature unusually lowering around her. She has been getting dragged to her dreams for the past many days. She is having unexplainable incidents happening with her and time overlapping through her dreams…

She remembers her childhood dreams…same place, same people…this place…

A sudden realization jolts her whole body up with the highest intensity…the first time she dreamt of these stairs, the first time she met her friend here…with each dream, the character changed…the girl grew up…just like she did…that girl grew up in her dreams…

"You never lose any of your dreams…all are there to become your reality," the unnaturally light voice starts fading up as she feels like she is slipping inside a coma.

"Your reality is your another dream…illusion…wake up to live the rest…."

Nia feels extremely light and frozen…like a diminishing star in the galaxy…fading up for an eternity.

"Where do the dreams go? They don't go anywhere…they take you to where you belong."

Sumedha looks at the lifeless face of Nia. Another hypnosis…another death…another birth of a new dream…in someone's eyes. A smile creeps on her face.

<hr>

5

"You go and bring the ball today," Aaden says to the boy who has just hit the window of the yellow house. The ball went straight inside shattering the glass.

The boy wearing the same white shirt runs towards the house, Aaden feels good looking at them…they are such good friends of his…

Soon a ball drops near his feet… he looks up at the house as he finds the girl saying with anger, "If it happens again, I will keep you all locked inside."

"Sorry, di!" Aaden apologizes looking at the angry face of the girl standing like a frozen mannequin near the window.

Nia sighs, as she goes inside…the room….or another dream.

The Last Night's Party

There is something about late-night parties- the ambience, vibe, and feelings. It's like a glimpse of some hidden universe within our known one, it's a place where our lost expectation may blossom again and something out-of-the-world can happen, just like that. Ritiksha was sitting on a couch and having drinks comfortably while watching out around her. It was her third shot and more to go. The dance floor was not only for dancing but to her, it was something stories were born from. So many people, so many different types of dance, and so many stories to divulge. Ritiksha's eyes and soul were hungry to get more of this. As soon as she made herself comfortable on the couch from the sweltering heat outside, she found herself getting a shot of Bacardi. As it drenched her mouth and throat and travelled downwards, she felt a sense of relaxation, like she had been seeking it for long. She made herself comfortable on one of the couches as she started observing around her. It had been more than an hour now. Though she was dressed up in a black short bodycon dress and stiletto, fully ready to set fire on the dance floor as anyone would think, she kept sitting only. She started feeling a bit dizzy after a point in time and she liked it so much. The dim lights above her head were getting blurred in and out as she kept staring at them unblinkingly, feeling high. Someone from far was watching her since the time she took the seat. The person was observing her every move, how she was sipping the drink touching her dark red lips at the edge of the glass, she was occasionally moving her fingers through her side locks and widening her eyes as if to keep herself awake. She seemed to be calm and enjoying the music, but she didn't budge from her place, not even shook her shoulder with the beats for once, and yet she seemed the loudest one to catch the attention, at least to the person watching her. Her eyes were scanning everyone on the dance floor and yet she looked the least interested in showing some moves. Her eyes were shining and as she tilted her head to one side after her fourth shot, both her eyes looked like they were holding a bright star in each. She crossed her legs which were glistening in the dim lights from above her head and her glittery black dress looked even shorter as she bent backwards to leave herself on the couch to relax fully. The person couldn't wait further. It was time to make a move.

Ritiksha was almost feeling the drinks through her veins as she finished the fifth shot and half-immersed herself on the couch. The cocktail of lights, music, crowd, dance, Bacardi, and unknown fragrances was making her high and she didn't want the feeling to fade out. It was like a pool of sensations she was sinking in, and yet she was fully conscious. She thought of getting a lemonade before starting the next round. And then she sensed something…something she didn't want at all. The guy ordered drinks as he sat beside her. She wanted to get up and sit at some distance but was too lazy to do so. She kept staring in front of her flooded with music and lights. It was not the time to go yet. It was her night…all of it…hers only. Her head started feeling heavy gradually and she left herself on the couch, but with full control over herself. The intense fragrance was making her a bit uncomfortable as she sensed the person beside her was about to make a move. But she chose to stay silent and let it be.

'Hey! You alright?' a sharp yet soft voice came from beside her.

'Yes! I am!' she answered in a softer tone without looking at the person. The cacophony of the night was fading in the background as the intense perfume and the slight brush of his hand near her elbow made her conscious. The guy took the seat in front of her, maybe to make it easier for her to look at him, he was right. Ritiksha observed the tall, fair, well-built, handsome guy in front of her, he was in the middle of his 20s. He had a drink in his hand but was yet to take a sip from it. He only looked at her once or twice while checking out around him. He seemed to be decent to not poke her too much or try to start a conversation, yet desperate enough to get what he came for. Ritiksha liked the situation, and for the first time since the evening, she gave some of her attention to him from observing the people on the dance floor, without him noticing it.

'Do you know, every leap year one murder happens in this pub?' Ritiksha got shocked by the suddenness and type of question she was asked. She couldn't decide instantly how to show her nonchalance, but in the next moment she tackled it swiftly, 'Not really…not much interested though. Just relaxing,' Ritiksha tried to sound as casual as she could and wanted him to know she was habituated with coming across such situations where even more handsome guys try to make unsuccessful moves. The guy frowned a bit, but he was a skilful player. 'Well…it is said…alternately it's a man and woman who gets murdered every leap year. Isn't that…' he stopped for a while to choose the correct words, 'Interesting?' his eyes shone and he looked even more dashing in that navy blue shirt folded near his biceps, 'You can Google if you don't believe,' he shrugged. Ritiksha liked how he was eager to get her talk and she was the least interested in checking the facts and information. That night she just wanted to let it be, and experience all of it. Ritiksha only tilted her headto one side, threw him a look and then looked around her. She felt the buzz was fading and this time she went over to get herself another drink, the guy watched her for a while and then settled in. Ritiksha finished her shot in one go and then came back to her place, it was still empty, but she was not sure how long it would be as she could sense a lot of girls were eyeing him.

'Let's play a game?' Ritiksha spoke this time.

'What?' he asked throwing his hands in the air. He looked amused, surprised, and playful at the same time.

Ritiksha crossed her legs and leaned a bit forward, 'I will ask you to name the most unexpected thing you are capable to do and you will show me doing it.' She kept a straight face as she ordered a plate of chicken fries. Her concentration was back at everything but him.

'Done!' he leaned back on the seat as if the ball was in his court.

Ritiksha smiled inside. 'Well, can I dare you to do one thing right now?' She took a bite of the chicken fry, it was hot and spicy, her tongue craved some water, but she let it be. The guy nodded as his eyes sparkled. 'You say, anything.'

'Kiss a guy on his lips,' Ritiksha answered promptly. She didn't know where did it come from but didn't feel like correcting or changing it. Ritiksha only met his eyes for a second before concentrating back on her fries. The guy smirked as he left his seat and approached the dance floor. And Ritiksha couldn't help getting impressed seeing what happened in the next few minutes. It all happened so fast…it took hardly 10 minutes for him to go to the dance floor with smoothness and kiss right on the lips of that lean, fair guy wearing ripped jeans and an oversized t-shirt. He was gay. For the first time, she noticed him. She had been piercing the crowd since the evening so she couldn't have missed him. He must have entered just then. Not only did the guy kiss and dance with him, but he also bid him goodbye too soon, all so smoothly and in a timely manner that she wondered whether he set it up all beforehand. But it was not possible, she knew.

'Well done,' she said as he came back.

'What's next?' Ritiksha shrugged. Her plate was already empty and she felt quite full, but the night just started for her, she could say.

'Show me the most vulnerable side of yours!' she said as she opened her tiny mirror to touch up her red lips, she didn't care to use the washroom to touch up, she was comfortable enough.

'Whoa! Isn't it your turn?' He looked surprised.

'Turn? Really? Did I say that ever? The game is for you only!'

Ritiksha's sharp look pierced his eyes. Her face and big eyes which were looking even bigger in her mascara were enough to intoxicate anyone, he thought.

'Cool! Won't mind!' he said while he knew there was more to the game, and definitely, it was not one-sided.

'Show it!'

'What?' He looked a bit disappointed yet enthusiastic.

'Well, show me one side of yours you are proud of.'

Before she could say or hear further, he came and leaned kissing her left cheek, 'Audacity,' he spoke in her ear, it was not a whisper, yet it made her shiver a bit. Inside, she didn't expect it at all, but she kept calm, 'We should leave! Playing the game in the same place makes it boring!' she got up as if she had something in her mind. He followed her with a brief nod and smile. He was definitely up for more!

When they got inside the cab, it was nearly midnight. So far the game had been interesting, the guy, whose name was still unknown to her, had already done several stunts and Ritiksha was quite impressed with how smoothly he pulled off everything. 'Care to show me your weakness?' she asked in such a voice, only he could hear it.

'Didn't I skip the question?'

'For the time being, but now is the time to attend it. You can't drop any question off,' she spoke. 'Or, the game will lose its charm!'

The night was getting darker outside and she felt the excitement rising in her.

'Oh!' The guy took a few seconds as if to think whether he should quit the game or not. And just then something happened. The car in front of them halted with upside-down screeching loudly before lying lifeless ahead of them in the next few seconds. The roads were empty apart from a few other bigger cars and a lorry which all passed by that car. None stopped and no one could be seen anywhere nearby. The cab driver stopped the cab and went out to see the matter. Ritiksha swallowed, the guy also got down from the cab and joined the driver. Ritiksha wanted to go, but somehow she kept sitting inside. She called the emergency number, but there was no network. After waiting for some time, she opened the cab door and came out. Only the tall street lights were standing aloof, she couldn't find anyone in her sight. The car was lying in a shadowy place, a bit far from where she was standing and she couldn't see anything clear from there. She didn't know the road she was in, but it was deserted and silent. She called the emergency number again as she stepped towards the car, but there was no network yet. 'Strange!' she muttered under her breath as she looked around. The excitement with which she started playing the game disappeared like vapour and she badly wanted to go back to her place. While thinking all this, she didn't notice when she came near the car. Even the flashlight was not working on her mobile. 'Damn it!' she took a few steps forward, from outside she could find the outlines of the people stuck inside. She couldn't see any of the guys or the driver and understood that they went for help. She tried to call multiple numbers, but there was no network at all. The road she was standing in, seemed too long to find its end or other roads. It had been more than 10-15 minutes that the guy and the driver were gone. Ritiksha gained the courage to look inside this time. One side of the car was visible in the streetlights and as she tried to look inside through the broken window of the upside-down car. Her heart jumped in shock and horror, it started beating so fast that she felt like having a heart attack at any moment. The streetlights were amalgamated with the bloodstream flooding through the navy blue shirt, and his eyes were still staring at her, shining and alive.

The Dream Date

1

"How am I looking?" Eva enters the room with her dazzling smile. She is looking ravishing in the cherry red gown.

"You are looking okay!" Adah says, without looking up, her eyes are glued to the book.

"At least look at me before you answer!" Eva says, irritated, rolling her eyes.

"You are looking okay," Adah looks at her through her thick glasses for a few seconds and then concentrates on her study again.

"Thank you!" Eva says mockingly and leaves the room.

"Will you come back today?" Adah asks her shouting.

There is no answer. She hears the loud sound of the main gate being closed.

How will I make her understand?' she thinks, disappointed.

After a long time, Eva feels that old vibes in her—carefree, happy and excited! She has always imagined a date night like this. It's their second meeting only and he has already read her mind to do as per her wishes to make her happy.

"Wow! You look beautiful," Rohit says looking at her with his mesmerized eyes. He opens and holds the car door for her.

"Thank you!" Eva says while tucking the hair behind her ear which was falling on her eyes in the cold evening breeze. There is a tuneful silence around them apart from the light sound of the wind, the few dots of the house-lights far away are getting off one by one. Being on the hilly side, people here still sleep early, the shopping malls and restaurants shut by 10 at night as well. "And thanks for all," she says smiling while getting inside the car, breathing in the beautiful moments.

"More to come…thank me then," Rohit says with a mischievous smile, his eyes shining like a moonlit dream waiting to embrace her with all his love and warmth.

Rohit gets in and sits beside her, ready to take her to his drive full of surprises yet to come. His hand brushes against hers as he starts the car, Eva feels a tingling sensation all over her, the goose-bumps are telling her to hold on till the surreal moments arrive.

Her mobile starts ringing at this very moment flashing the name 'Adah.' She disconnects the call, irritated. A message pops up in the next moment from Adah, it reads-

'You really think you got the man of your dreams? So easily? Out of nowhere? Listen, anything too good to be true, is often not good at all, but the opposite…you still have time…'

Eva's mood drops a bit reading the message. She closes the message without replying.

Another message pops in the next moment-

'Use your brain or you are gonna regret…'

Eva switches off her mobile, to get rid of the messages for the time being.

"All good?" Rohit asks while driving quietly. He is observing the change of her mood for quite a few minutes.

The car is sliding through the moonlit silent, beautiful roads, leaving the houses behind…

"No, nothing. It's just my sister," she says looking at the rain-soaked view, tinged with the silver moonlight. "She worries too much."

"No problem! It's alright," Rohit squeezes her hand assuringly. "This dress suits you," he says, smiling, looking at her brown eyes. "I love the color," he adds looking at her smiling eyes. "You are too pretty…inside and out."

Eva smiles. Her face turns crimson.

2

"Will you listen for a minute?" Adah tries to talk politely.

"Ssshhhh," Eva gestures to her with a finger on her lips, the mobile pressed in her ear. She slowly shifts herself at a distance, so that Adah can't hear the conversation.

Adah can't believe she is ignoring her like this!

"You have to listen to me right now!" Adah says shouting. "The guy you are in love with is cheating on you!"

Eva pauses for a second as she looks confused. "What the hell!" Eva hangs up the call as she faces her sister, "I know him well. Stop shouting!" She observes the expression on her sister's face. "What did he think?! You were shouting like a madcap! I know him better than you!" she says angrily, irritated and shocked by her sister's resistance.

"No you don't! Some of my friends…" Adah tries to convince her.

"He has changed Adah. Relax…" Eva says and leaves the room.

Eva comes to the large patio and calls Rohit. Her mood is off and she just needs to take her mind off it. Her heart skips a beat as the familiar ringtone of his mobile starts ringing, very near to her. She looks around, her eyes searching curiously. In the very next moment, two strong hands wrap her from her behind as the hypnotic fragrance envelops her senses followed by a feather-light whisper, "I have a surprise for you…come with me!" She feels an instant longing to follow the words. Her mood is already better, and she feels ecstatic and curious at the same time as she turns around to look into Rohit's sincere gaze, lovingly staring at her.

-But…Adah…" she tries to speak.

"Will manage," Rohit says and holds her hand. She feels all the warmth of his love in his clutch.

3

Eva takes her steps forward as he wraps his hands around her waist. As she climbs down the stairs in front of her patio, she looks back once at their house, all the windows are closed and thankfully Adah is not peeking from one of those. His silver color car is parked just in front of their house. It has absorbed all the shine from the Full Moon, scattering the silver shades around the cold, deserted endless roads, a few clouds can be seen far from here near the hazy hilltops…the whole world seems to be sleeping, while only two of them keep walking, inundated in the moonlight.

As soon as they get inside the car, Rohit gives her a bouquet of Roses, the fresh fragrance of the dark red roses gives her an instant high. She smiles silently looking at his sparkling eyes, it's like she can catch all the brightness of this moonlit night looking at his smiling eyes. He bends slightly towards her and plants a soft kiss on her cheek making her shiver inside for a few seconds. She hears some whimpering coming from the backseat. Rohit tucks a few strands of her hair behind her ear and starts the car, his eyes glued to her. She can see so much passion in his eyes getting intense like a glowing flame. The roads are running behind with the increasing speed of the car, those look surreal in the silver moonlight. Eva feels a sudden coldness touching her fingers wrapped around the roses.

She hears the same whimpering coming just from inside the car. Rohit is driving, his gaze fixed in front. Suddenly she feels something is wrong there. As she checks her mobile, she finds no network at all. She feels the stinging coldness moving from her fingertips to her wrists. Her heart starts beating loudly in her ears, she feels numb and nauseous looking at the red of the roses dripping down from all its petals, making those colorless and white…the same sound from some unknown source is growing louder, it's just behind her ears…a few seconds away from touching her. Eva feels her whole body is frozen and stuck in the seat of the car, her voice has been snatched away and her eyelids don't exist. Rohit is looking at her. His eyes look sinister. Within a fraction of a second, his body starts changing…to…something…she can't believe…

Her heart is acting so weird that it can stop at any time. The glowing moonlight is sucking out all her senses…before the whole world around her collapses into the darkness…she remembers only one face…her beloved sister Adah.

An Afternoon Away

1

"Are you done with your packing?" Sophia asks looking at her luggage.

"Yes, I am done!" Ritika says proudly looking at her through the mirror while drying her hair.

"Alright!" Sophia looks at the large trollies all kept neatly at the corner of the room, "I will take a nap. Wake me up before you leave," she says throwing herself on the bed. Her eyelids are heavy after a long, hectic night shift.

"Sure!" Ritika says with a light smile on her face, as she combs her long hair.

It's a beautiful afternoon. The blazing sunlight making its way through the white net curtains is making some floral patterns on the marble floor. Ritika can't wait for her journey to start!

2

"Don't forget to call me once you reach!" Ritika's mother says wiping the corner of her eyes while watching her younger daughter leave for two long years. Time flies so fast! And her daughters never stop making her proud. She looks at her smiling. Ritika comes and hugs her tightly. "Don't worry, ma. I will take care. Love you!" she says again, smiling with a bit of heaviness in her heart. For the first time, she will be staying for so long and so far away from her family. She is damn excited to have the new life of her dreams abroad, and at the same time, she knows how much she is gonna miss her family!

Ritika hugs her dad as he wishes her all the best cheering her up and then her elder sister kisses her cheeks saying, "Take care Ritu! Get some hot guy there and send both of your pics to me soon!" she says with a notorious smile winking at her grown-up sister.

"Sure I will!" Ritika whispers laughing. She bids all goodbye with excitement, and a slightly heavy heart as she approaches the entrance of the airport.

3

"Has she picked up?" Mrs. Paul asks, tensed.

"No!" Sophia shakes her head as she calls her number again. "She is supposed to reach by now," she says pressing the mobile to her ear. Her mom is eagerly waiting for an update, she already looks tense.

Sophia keeps calling her number. It's not reachable. She is worried a bit, somehow she doesn't feel everything is fine. Her flight is supposed to land by this time, it's been several hours in fact. Ritika boarded the flight on time and she never delayed in informing home as needed. Their mother has anxiety issues and she had severe anxiety attacks in the past triggered by various reasons. All their family members, especially both the daughters take care so that it doesn't happen again.

After trying to contact for several times, Sophia comes back to her room, she thinks of letting her call back as and when she wants. Maybe she got busy with something. Her mother is speaking with someone in the next room. Her dad is yet to return from his workplace. She tried again for the last couple of times, it says the number doesn't exist! Strange!

Sophia leans on the sofa while scrolling through her emails as she starts replying to the pending ones.

Her mobile starts ringing with the familiar ringtone flashing the picture of both the sisters.

"Hello Ritu!" Sophia says, relaxed. "Where are you now?" She walks towards the drawing hall, her dad has just returned from the office, he is talking with her mom about something.

Sophia looks at them and nods to assure them as she tries to hear what she is saying. There is some constant noise from the other side.

"I have just reached and I am fine!" Ritika says in her cheerful voice.

"Your flight delayed?" she asks walking towards the balcony to get a better network.

"No, it didn't! Good morning! And I will just call in sometime!" Ritika says hurriedly as she hangs up before Sophia could talk further.

But morning?! It's supposed to be night there,' Sophia thinks, a bit confused.

A few hours pass, Ritika doesn't call back. Neither can they contact her as it keeps saying the number doesn't exist.

After another long wait, Sophia's mobile rings flashing her sister's number. But it shows 'unknown' instead of showing her name or picture.

"Hi! What's up?" Sophia asks as she leans on the railing in her balcony looking at the city lights near and far.

"I couldn't reach the apartment!" Ritika says shouting, her voice sounds scared and anxious.

"It's just ten minutes away from the airport! Alex didn't give you the direction?" Sophia asks, confused. "What's going on there? Can you tell?" she asks, concerned.

"I have been walking for the last two hours!" Ritika shouts again. Her voice is shaking a bit.

"What?" Sophia asks, shocked. "Why didn't you just take a cab in the first place? And why didn't you connect to him or your flat owner at least?!" she says angrily, she just can't get why is her sister behaving weirdly since she left home!

"There is not a single person or creature around me! Let alone taking a cab!" Ritika says from the other side, she sounds freaked out.

"You are in Sydney, Ritu! How is that even possible?!" Sophia says shouting as she shivers in the cold breeze standing on her balcony. Has her sister gone mad?

"Something is wrong!" she speaks in the same tone.

"There is no one here...when this journey will end?" she says in a choked voice.

"Okay, wait! Is there any building or restaurant or anything...anything near you?" Sophia tries to keep calm, as she struggles inside to find out what's happening there.

"No, nothing!" Ritika utters after a few seconds. "It's a beautiful dazzling day here…full of sunshine, rain-drenched roads…but…" she swallows. "It's completely deserted! It's…completely!" she speaks out the last few words unmindfully like she is doing something else.

"Just send me the location, fast!" Sophia says hurriedly. "Don't cut the line! It's not a prank right?" she asks even after knowing she won't do such stupid pranks.

"No! It's not…I am sending…right now…" Ritika's panic-stricken voice comes floating from the other side as the constant noise keeps amplifying rapidly.

"No location can be detected!" Ritika shouts from the other side.

"What? Listen…" Sophia tries to speak but in the next moment, she rushes inside the room as she hears both her parents are shouting. They look horrified as they gesture towards the TV.

Her eyes fall on the headlines while she struggles to hear Ritika on the other side-

The Flight DSL-303, Delhi to Sydney, has gone missing for last 18 hours. There is no trace of it till now…'

"Where the hell are you then?" Sophia asks, shouting, all scared and panicked.

There is no sound of her, only static noise. She rushes towards the balcony as she keeps shouting over the phone to talk to Ritika.

"Hello! Can you hear me?" Ritika's faint voice comes from far as she struggles to talk.

The line disconnects within the next few seconds.

Sophia calls her number immediately, panting. She can't hear what her parents are saying, she feels like her brain is not working.

The number you are trying to call does not exist.'

Sophia feels frozen and anxious…as some uninvited thought clouds her mind unexpectedly, even at this time!

Suddenly she remembers the research topic her sister took 'Overlapping of space and time in the forms of signals.'

She remembers that page of her research paper, which she called absurd-

'Crosstalk (the unwanted transfer of signals) is possible in the real life between time and space. And it is quite possible to be irreversible.'

Journey to the End

1

Avni looks at her watch again, her eyes on the entrance of the café.

'Are you coming?' she types and hits the send, looking around her restlessly. She is getting late for her classes.

After a few minutes, she finds the familiar face approaching her.

"Hey!" She looks up to meet the sleepless eyes in front of her.

"What's so urgent?" she asks looking at the pale face staring back at her from across the table. "And why aren't you in school uniform?" she asks again.

The person sitting opposite her smiles, shrugging off her all other questions as she fishes out a small red velvet box from her jeans pocket, she tries to smile again mysteriously as she speaks, "It's for you!"

The small red velvet box is held in front of her. A slice of sunlight falling on the top of it is making it all shiny.

-"Birthday gift!" Zara says beaming at her curious face.

"It was a month before!" Avni says looking at the twinkling pearl-like cherry red drop, as she opens the box. "What's this?" she asks looking at her smiling face.

"Something special," Zara winks with the same smile pasted on her face.

"Wow! Is that?" Avni asks observing the tiny stone held between her fingers, which is scattering a thin red-ray after absorbing the sunlight. "It must be some precious stone...you know its name?"

"Sure it is!" Zara says blinking her eyes once as she observes her friend's curious face.

"Okay! I have to leave!" Avni hurries as she checks the time. "I will miss school today if I don't go now!" she says as she takes her stuff from the table.

"Okay! I am visiting my aunt, so, will see you soon!" Zara hugs her and shortly they leave the café bidding each other goodbye.

2

It's just the first class, and Avni can't stop yawning. She feels like she hasn't slept for a decade as she tries to concentrate on the letters scribbled on the blackboard.

She keeps struggling throughout the whole class as the whole classroom seems to be fading in and out from her sight.

As soon as the bell rings, she rushes to the washroom, she opens the tap and sprinkles some water on her face coming near the washbasin. Her eyelids feel so heavy that she can sleep right there only. She keeps splashing water on her face to take her sleep away. As she opens her eyes to keep herself awake, she notices something terrible…her face looks drained of blood, her lips chapped. She shivers in shock and pain as she looks at her hands… her palms are full of eyelashes.

She comes back to the class, weaker, her body shaking in fear and shock. The next class has already started. With trembling hands, she starts copying the physics notes from the blackboard and something strikes her.

The law of conservation of energy- it can neither be created nor destroyed. Her tired eyes get stuck at the line *'It transforms from one form to another'* in her copy. A chill runs down her spine as she keeps her hand inside the pocket to find the velvet box. She can hear the silent echo of the same words in her mind, *'transforms…it transforms…'*

'From one form to another'…she feels dizzy as she murmurs, *'from one person to another.'*

The girl sitting next to her is looking at her.

'Are you okay?' she asks her.

Avni nods. She is scared.

"There is something for you…I forgot to give you!" Avni gives her the velvet box. "From my last trip," she feels guilty and helpless.

~~~~~~

Avni keeps walking ignoring all her tiredness, she needs to reach on time. She feels weak, but not scared anymore. She needs the whole story. She finds a crowd in front of Zara's house as she comes near it.

"What happened?" she asks a random middle-aged man. Her mouth feels dry, her voice sounds like a whisper.

"The girl Zara…she has died today…she went to meet her friend in the morning…but after coming back…"

Avni can't hear or see or feel anything, as her whole world starts getting dark sucking out all the leftover energy in her.
~~~~~~

Dim Lit Love

"I just don't want to go back today!" Prisha throws her hands in the air, her eyes half-shut.

Jiya takes a moment to observe her as she smiles, "Look who is saying!" She comes towards her and wraps her hand around her shoulder. "Really we should enjoy the last day of the year, together…"

"Yup! It's the last year of our college too!" Hansh squeezes himself between the two of them as he always does. "Let's go!"

"So what are you waiting for?" Eashan shrugs.

The whole car reverberates with the chirping sound of the young hearts vibrating in the happiness of celebrating the last year together! They always celebrate the last day of the year together since the first year of their college.

When they were in the first year and just became friends, that year Jiya's grandmother passed away in the month of December. She used to be so close to her grandmom and it broke her fully that time. She ended up isolating herself from the others. Prisha, Hansh and Eashan all went to visit her at her grandparent's farmhouse that year. They found her cold and shaking in distress in a corner of the vast empty house clutching her grandmother's belongings. The last one of her family to love her unconditionally as she says. She lost her parents when she was only 12 years old. And her grandfather left her grandmother just after her dad was born. She never saw his face even in the picture. After that day or incident, they became even closer and promised themselves to not leave each other for a lifetime no matter what. They spent one month in that farmhouse leaving all other work behind and finally celebrated the last day of the year with a smile on everyone's face.

"Are you ready guys?" Hansh says with a mischievous smile on his face as he presses the accelerator.

"Yes! We are!" Jiya shouts excitedly with her high-pitched voice as always.

Eashan looks at Prisha's half-sleepy face leaned on his shoulder, "She already looks exhausted…"

"We can drop her then," Sana says looking at them. She has just started hanging out with them, it's been a couple of months. Eashan seemed to be interested in her initially, but soon he realized that there is nothing else attractive in her apart from her looks. However, she kept hanging out with them as the rest of them jelled up with her quite well.

"Noo…nnoo…I am fine…I will go…" Prisha says in the next moment in her semi-drunk voice clutching Eashan's hand. Sana looks away.

"Okay…okay…cool," Jiya says in a soothing tone holding up her palms as her eyes scan all quickly. "All are going!" she taps on Hansh's shoulder, "Take a left turn from here!"

"I know the route baby!" he smirks as he keeps driving towards the same direction. "Screw your Google map!"

"Why aren't we going to any nearby place?!" Jiya says tapping her mobile.

Sana is humming a song while her eyes are dipped in the dense trees and houses sliding too fast backwards. The night is silent yet enjoyable, it's unlike the other parts of the city where every place is overflowing with high-volume music, wine, and people, cars and bikes flooding the streets, and people flaunting their high-street fashion. This is the first time that they are yet to be a part of that and Jiya is already feeling disappointed.

"It will be the best place ever! I promise!" Eashan says assuring the rest of them.

Prisha says something inaudible. Eashan wraps his hands around her waist as she leaves herself on him even more.

"Let's see!" Jiya says looking at them, still not convinced enough. The car is almost flying through the broad, smooth road. As far as her eyes can observe, there is no other car, not even a single dot of light is there visible from any house. *Isn't it weird for 31ˢᵗ night?*

In a city which never sleeps?!' she thinks, waiting eagerly to reach their destination.

2   *hours later...*

"Will anyone please tell me what the hell is going on?" Sana says, irritated.

"Nothing, you dumb!" Prisha says furrowing her brows. "Can't you just keep quiet? Just enjoy the ride!" she sounds even drunker than before.

"Just shut up! Stop blabbering you drunkard!" Sana shouts, her face looking angry as she vents out all the frustration of several things going on with her.

"You won't talk with her like this!" Eashan raises his voice, his eyes bloodshot. "I am telling you again!"

"Will you guys stop fighting for a moment?" Jiya says while trying to figure out something, she was talking with Hansh, "We are just stuck at the same place for the last 20 minutes!"

"I am asking that only!" Sana rolls her eyes. Her face looks dark and offended. "Hansh, what's the matter?" she taps his shoulder.

"There is no night club with this name here. Even the names of the streets are not matching suddenly, since we crossed the last stoppage of the city," Hansh says, his eyes glued to his mobile.

"Someone said to screw Google map!" Jiya says mockingly.

Prisha laughs loudly.

"I gave all the info to you guys," Hansh says. "You should have checked it too!"

"Why should we! While you can beat all the maps and all!" Sana taunts him.

"Just ask your friend again na!" Jiya says restlessly. Her eyes are scanning the secluded place they are stuck in. "See this place, who will say it's 31st night?" Jiya says.

"That's what happens when you crave free drinks!" Sana says, looking through the condensed dark around them…the few street lights look very powerless in front of the thick black surrounding their car. Eashan and Prisha look the least affected in the present condition. Eashan is whispering something in her ears, while she is murmuring and laughing which most probably is audible to him only.

"See this!" Eashan gives his phone to Hansh taking out a moment from their PDA. "It's the official page of the nightclub. Everything is given here."

"We have exactly followed the same route," Hansh shows him on the map. "But just after crossing the road, nothing can be matched with the original direction."

Eashan takes his mobile and observes intently, Prisha peeks in from beside him, pressing her cheeks on his shoulder.

"Hansh is right," Sana says looking at her mobile. "I am just clueless!"

"Let's ask someone!" Jiya says.

"Whom?" Eashan says looking around. "No one is here!"

"Well…just go back?" Jiya utters promptly.

All the faces turn towards her with a surprised look pasted there.

"Whatever!" Jiya shrugs. "Then find it!" she leans back on the seat.

"I think we should go back," Sana breaks the silence after a few minutes, while everyone is busy trying to figure it out separately.

"Sure?" Hansh turns around to face her.

"As if we have an option!" Sana says checking out Prisha once, who is busy checking her mobile, her face looks dipped in thoughts.

"All right!" Eashan speaks up. "Let's go back and enjoy at least before it's morning!"

Prisha looks up from her phone nodding at what he has said.

"Done!" Hansh says as he starts taking a U-turn. His face looks dark and devoid of any emotion.

After an hour...

"Why have you stopped?" Eashan asks looking up at Harsh. "Oh shit! It's a dead-end!"

-Waste of time!" Sana says, utterly irritated. "Find another way!"

"Ya!" Hansh says unmindfully.

But even after half an hour, they can't find any way out.

"Let's see if we can do anything!" Eashan gets out of the car.

"I will come too!" Prisha says, straightening herself up on the seat.

"No, you stay here," Eashan says, his eyes searching for something.

"Let me come with you!" Hansh gets down. "Rest can stay inside!"

"Okay! Don't take a decade to figure things out!" Jiya says tilting her head through the window.

She has already given up on tonight's plan and is trying to control her anger maintaining a straight face.

"So, you are still not out of that?" Prisha looks at Sana, piercing her with a sharp gaze.

"What?" Sana says, a bit unprepared with the sudden question.

"That Eashan rejected you!"

Sana keeps quiet for some seconds and then slaps hard on her face.

After half an hour more...

"I think something is wrong," Hansh says. "Can you call Shina and ask her? She stays near this road you said."

"Yes, but I don't have her number. We chat only." Eashan replies promptly.

"It's absurd, but really we are trapped," Hansh says as they walk towards the car.

There is only Jiya standing outside.

"They started a fight and got down," Jiya says with a dark face. "I tried to stop…but…they…just…I don't know where they are!" She holds her head with her hands.

"What?" Eashan looks at her, utterly shocked and calls Prisha's number in the next moment.

As it starts ringing, all get startled at the very moment as the sound seems to be coming from the back of the car.

All of them start approaching the source of the sound, confused, curious and scared. Eashan has kept the mobile pressed to his ears, his heart in his mouth, beating louder than anything.

The sound is coming from the trunk of the car.

Hansh opens it with his slightly trembling hands.

Jiya screams in horror in the very next second. Eashan sits on the road with a thud losing control of everything. Hansh can't move an inch in shock and terror.

All the pairs of eyes keep staring with horror at the lifeless body of Prisha laying right in front of them…Hansh holds his trembling fingers close to her nose to only get confirmation of the harrowing nightmare standing right in front of them.

The loud sound of Eashan's mobile comes floating to their ears…messages are popping one after another in his mobile.

Jiya approaches the mobile which is laying far from Eashan…on the empty road.

Her trembling fingers click on it, her mind is blank like an empty blackboard.

There are uncountable Facebook messages popping up from a profile named 'Shina'.

She holds the mobile in front of Eashan's eyes, who has stopped reacting to anything and is staring like a statue.

The message reads-

'Had a very great time with you on the way. Right now with Sana. Will come back once I am done with my work.

YOU ARE MINE.'

Eashan clicks on the profile name like a robot.

The last post is from 5 years ago.

He never saw it before, it reads-

'REST IN PEACE.'

Looks Like You

1

"Wow! Such a beautiful view!" Mahek exclaims happily as her blindfold gets removed from her eyes.

"You like it?" Aaron says looking at her, concerned, his hands still holding hers.

She nods, smiling looking at the twinkling skyline beyond the tall buildings of the bustling city, her eyes shining like the tiny flames of candles.

"Okay, now relax!" Aaron says wrapping his hand around her waist. "You have the rest of your life to enjoy this view!" He plants a soft kiss on her forehead looking at the happy face of his wife.

She hugs him silently with tears in her eyes. After a decade she can breathe in so lightly and joyfully with her man by her side. Aaron hugs her tightly taking away her worries and anxiety-like absorbing the dark cold night by the only warmth of the blazing fireplace. His mobile rings shortly and he excuses himself. "Just a moment…you look around, I will be back," he says looking at the name of his boss flashing on his mobile screen. "I will just be back! Having an urgent call."

"Alright," Mahek says nodding. "Will wait," she adds looking at him walking away as she sighs.

As Aaron goes out of her sight, she looks at the scratches and cut marks on her hand. She averts her eyes quickly, *'How could I?'* She closes her eyes as she can almost feel the fresh pain those cut marks gave her. In the next moment, her mobile rings breaking the chain of her thoughts- another appointment with her doctor. She cuts the call instantly.

She takes a few more steps along the large, long balcony with the strings of yellow bright lights wrapped in its railing…it should be at least $14^{th}/15^{th}$ floor. She doesn't know exactly. She was blindfolded the whole way. She comes to the large drawing room decorated beautifully with lights and fresh flowers. She is feeling lighter and joyous after a long time.

Mahek visits all the rooms one by one. It's too beautiful. She can't believe it is all theirs to live and enjoy the rest of their lives.

She looks at the big clock in the drawing-room, it's 8 p.m. She opens her side bag quickly, she got late- she fishes out the strip of tablets and gulps down one with the water.

As she keeps roaming inside the big apartment, she looks for Aaron. But he can't be seen anywhere.

She sits on the sofa waiting for him to come back to her. The whole apartment is beautifully furnished. She switches on the TV to keep herself busy until he comes back.

As soon as the TV turns on, her mouth falls open in surprise. She can't believe her eyes! She covers her mouth with both hands as her eyes stare back at the most memorable event of her life!

She can't resist calling him there instantly. She calls his number, keeping her eyes on their wedding video. It's unreachable.

She puts back the mobile on the table and makes herself more comfortable on the sofa while waiting for him to turn up with more surprises.

Few hours later...

Mahek searches for her blanket, her eyes still closed. She is curled up on the sofa in cold. There is a whisper in her ears saying something inaudible. She wakes up with a jolt, her eyes wide open. There is no one. Only the discrete sound of water droplets falling somewhere nearby is echoing in the room. She slowly stands up as she calls Aaron by his name, her eyes searching for him in all directions. The sound of her own voice comes back to her piercing the thick, condensed silence. She hears the sound coming from the kitchen. The whole apartment is submerged in the darkness, there is no light anywhere inside. Her hands find the switchboard in that darkness, but none of the switches seems to work. *'It must be power cut,'* she thinks. In the flashlight of her mobile, she finds her way towards the kitchen. *'Oh! There he is!'*

Aaron and everything around him are soaked in the semi-darkness. He seems to be cooking there with all his attention.

"Aaron!" she calls his name while approaching him. "I was searching for you…"

He doesn't respond instantly and turns towards her in the next moment and…

Mahek freezes at the same spot she was standing, unable to move or speak further. *'Again it's happening!'* she screams in fear and panic. The face in front of her is staring at her unblinkingly. It's not him fully, but yet it's no one but him. The face has his eyes, but other features are not fully like him. She wants to run towards him to save herself. But at the same time, she wants to run away from the part of him scaring her. As she takes a few more steps forward in a trance, her eyes fall on the thing he has just fished out from somewhere. The silver color object is glistening in the fading light. It's a knife. She wants to run, but her feet get tangled with some wire-like thing. And she falls on the floor with a thud.

2

Aaron drives as fast as he can as soon as he gets the news. Reaching home he presses the doorbell until the caretaker opens the door.

~~~~~~

He heaves a sigh of relief as the doctor tells him she is fine. She is still sleeping. Aaron drags a chair near her bed as he keeps an eye on her. His thought starts traversing a different era, the beautiful starting of their story. The doctor is still saying something before leaving the room. He can only hear some fragmented parts of his speech…some familiar words…

'needs more time.'

'rare combination.'

'fregoli syndrome'

'Schizophrenia'

'delusional belief'
~~~~~~

At the same time he can't help thinking about the person resembling him, the last time he appeared, she was sick for days…and no one has any clue about what happened. And this time…was it the caretaker or someone else? He wonders. He remembers what Mahek said in his ears, *I can be sick…but it's someone like you…maybe a part of yours lurking in the darkness of this house and only appears when you are not here.'*

Can he believe her words?

Walking Backwards

1

"Yes Sir! This one?" The salesgirl points out a thick, brown book with her long manicured figure.

"Yes please!" Sameer waits impatiently while she fetches it for him.

"Here it is!" she gives the book to him with a sweet smile.

Sameer fishes out the mobile from his pocket and reads the message again. Then he tells her to pack it quickly.

When he leaves the shop, it's almost evening. The area looks a bit deserted compared to the other days. There is a school and a lot of coaching centers nearby and almost all of those are closed now. As board exams are going on, the schools get emptied by afternoon as well.

Sameer puts the thick gift-paper-wrapped box in his backpack and texts Neha.

'Got it. First edition. 😊 *'*

Almost instantly her reply pops up.

'Okay. Come soon! I am ready!'

Sameer smiles, as he starts his bike.

"You know, Priya will be too happy seeing this birthday gift," Neha says smiling at him through the mirror, as she adjusts her neckpiece. She is glowing like anything in the off-while sleeveless salwar suit, the pearl neckpiece seems to be just made for her.

"Sure she will!" Sameer says smiling back at her. He can't take his eyes off her, she is looking even prettier than before! Or that's what he thinks while visiting her every three months!

"When will you return?" Sameer asks her as he keeps his wristwatch on the side table.

"Before 10 for sure!" Neha takes her clutch and the gift box. "You could have come with me!" she says looking at her husband who will get too impatient even if she is ten minutes late, she knows!

"I need to finish my work by tonight baby!" he says wrapping his hands around her shoulder. "Tomorrow is the last day here, I don't want to keep any work!" he says kissing her cheeks.

"Okay!" Neha smiles and bids him goodbye with a chaste kiss. "Have your dinner on time!" she says as she approaches the main gate leaving behind their rooms full of her fragrance.

Sameer wakes up with a jolt as the sharp sound of the doorbell hits him out of nowhere. He slept late and was sleeping like a dead until this utterly irritating sound woke him up fully!

Sameer gets up and opens the door in his half-sleepy eyes to find Neha standing with her reddened eyes and tensed face. He realizes that she didn't return home yesterday, neither did he wake up from his short nap of one hour!

"What happened?" he asks. She is looking so unlike her.

"There is something terribly wrong with Priya!" she utters in a shaking and scared tone. "I need to go again…I am taking the car…you…"

"I am coming with you too!" Sameer says quickly without a hint of what's exactly going on.

"No…I will tell you if I need. You need to stay here at home," she says hurriedly while about to go back to the car. "Will tell you everything…"

She leaves in their car in the next few seconds leaving a confused and clueless Sameer behind in the empty house.

"Son, I think it's affecting her too." His wrinkled face looks worried and concerned.

"What?" Sameer looks at Neha's dad, shocked to hear the tone of his voice. "What do you mean by affecting her?"

Sameer stands up from the sofa and walks towards her room. She is sleeping after taking the pill. Her parents' house is just half an hour away from their new home and she often spends a lot of time here when Sameer is away from home for his work. She lost her mom a year ago, just after their marriage. It was tragic. And she got kind of vulnerable since that time which made her stay back near her Dad's house while he is away for his work. He was all set to change his job for her but she made sure that he doesn't settle for less just to keep an eye on her. She is a beautiful paradox of being delicate and strong.

"Just one more year…and we can stay together only. I don't want you to sacrifice your career for getting a transfer one year earlier," she told him confidently. "I will be fine!"

And he agreed.

"I mean it," her dad says in an unusually dark voice.

"She is asleep…she is fine!" Sameer says looking at her. "And I don't believe that a book…" he says in desperation. The things going on are still incomprehensible to him and he just can't accept that she is in danger just like that!

"The first edition of the book was published in 1778. And the book you bought was published in 1773. Five years before the actual book!" her dad says, stating some facts. His voice sounds cold and devoid of emotion to him. Sameer looks at his wife once and then at the packed luggage that is kept near the sofa. At this time they were supposed to be at the airport. Sameer planned a surprise vacation for them for three days. We think one thing and life gives us something else…and often that is unwanted…isn't it?

"I don't get it!" Sameer says even without trying to dig in it.

The whole thing is happening in front of him like a bad dream, and somehow he is feeling the same negative vibe the old man is trying to convey to him.

He looks back at him with the same thought in his eyes.

Next morning…

Sameer wakes up late, his hands still clutching the dress she was wearing yesterday. He gets up with a jolt, all alert, as his eyes scan across the room. He was lying beside her and looking at her while waiting for everything to be normal again. He doesn't know when he fell asleep, clutching her.

In the next one hour, he searches for her in every possible place, calls to everyone known to her…but all in vain. She is nowhere. Her mobile is kept on the side table as it was when she went to sleep yesterday. It's like she has vanished overnight.

Sameer sits on the sofa, exhausted. Her dad has just entered the room, his face devoid of any expression. Sameer doesn't know where he was or whether he has any clue regarding what's happening. He feels so tired and directionless to ask anything, only hopes for Neha to come to him.

"The book you bought is a book written backwards," he stands near the window. "It's a story of the journey from everything to nothing," he speaks without looking at him even once. "The person who starts reading it joins the journey of the story written in this book in his/her own way. The person has to travel backwards…"

"What does that mean?" Sameer gets up to face him. "It doesn't make any sense. You must know where she is," Sameer says looking at his blank wrinkled face, exasperated.

"That means, the person has to travel from the present state to the one when he/she didn't exist…before being born you can say," he says like a machine without averting his gaze from him. "Priya has gone like this and..."

"Neha too!?" he can't believe himself saying this. He feels like his brain has stopped working.

He hears Neha's dad speaking-

"It's a cursed book which caused the disappearance of 57 people in the middle of the eighteenth century. Neha had an accident five years. She got a mild burn mark on her left hand, yesterday morning it became visible again," he whispers his last sentence. "And I knew her journey has started. She is gone..." he says in a trembling voice, as he leaves the room.

Three months later...

Sameer picks up the call to get rid of the continuous ringing. It's irritating him after the long sleepless night.

-Hello?" he speaks lightly.

"Am I speaking to Mr. Sameer Singh?" An aged voice asks from the other side. "Well, do you know where to find Mr. Ashok Trivedi? Your father-in-law?"

"No...he disappeared...it's been more than three months," he says matter-of-factly. "Who are you?"

"Well, I am Mr. Sanjeev Paul, his lawyer. We need to meet as soon as possible regarding the will his wife made…which says after 2 years 4 months of her death the whole property will be donated to the orphanage. And well, Mr. Ashok Trivedi had made the whole property in the name of his wife earlier."

"Is there any clause in that will, like, only in the absence of her spouse or daughter it will be done?"

"No…there isn't any," the answer comes promptly. "Can you let me know when…"

Sameer cuts the call in the midway, as the unsettlement spreads over him rapidly…

And there is no one to answer anymore…

Some answers only create more questions…the unanswerable ones…

The Painting

John throws the bag on the bed after coming back from school. He shouts for food as he leaves himself on the bed, still in his school dress.

"Can I ask you something?" He finds his grand-mom standing near his study table, lost in her thoughts. She hasn't scolded him for getting in the bed in his school dress today.

"Yup say!" he says turning towards her, half-lying.

"Is this yours?" She shows him his drawing copy.

John nods.

"Is this drawing yours?" she shows him a particular page. "Did you draw this?"

"Yes!" he says looking at her trembling hands, clueless.

She mumbles something and leaves the room. He can't understand anything.

Her body starts quivering in anticipation as she turns over the page to find the next picture. The smiling face of the boy which John painted is too lively like soon he will call her and come running to her to get in her lap.

And a chill runs down her spine as she remembers everything about the boy.

It's the picture of John's elder brother Alex. He died 1 year after John's birth.

And John has never seen his face, not even in any picture.

Beyond the Moon

Jasmine closes the book as she finishes reading it. It's 1:30 am, and as usual, she is not even a bit sleepy.

She is wide awake like this, for the last three days. She gets up from the bed and slowly walks towards the window. It's a beautiful view outside.

She looks at the moon-drenched garden with her insomniac big eyes. There is an unusual silence surrounding her. Slowly she approaches the door walking through her dark room where only a silvery trail of moonlight has made the path for her.

She tries to open the door, it's locked from outside. She feels dizzy. She is locked in this room for the last three days. And surprisingly, she didn't feel the need to go outside that much. She is feeling like she is floating in the subconscious, all the time.

There is one truth out of all these delusional feelings-she couldn't get over his absence…it's been two months or more. She never will…

She takes the book near her chest and inhales deeply. His last gift to her. It bears his fragrance. She can sense the fragrance getting intense with each passing moment…like he is very near to her.

She keeps the book on the table and stands near the window again. There is a shadow on the narrow pebble road in the garden.

And in the next moment…something occurs to her. She knows it's him.

All her senses become alert…waiting for an impossible to happen.

And…

It happens….

Too quickly, and too gently.

She feels like a feather…

~~~~~~

At the same time, on the terrace of that house – Rachel, Jasmine's sister finds something surreal happening in front of her eyes.

Two shadows in the garden are transforming into a single entity. With disbelief in her eyes, she witnesses the unison of the eternities.

She can't forgive herself for keeping the sleeping pills on the bedside table. She can't forgive herself for
~~~~~~

leaving her those few hours all alone. She can't stop blaming herself for the death of her only sister-Jasmine.

The Girl Behind the Book

Ankush stumbles on the huge bag kept near his feet as he rushes towards the seat. He hears a giggle.

Finally, he has managed to get a proper seat from where he can see those pair of eyes —dark, deep and expressive. He looks around again only to catch a glimpse of those dreamy eyes behind the cover of the book.

'Before I Sleep' He reads the title of the book he is least interested in.

He can see the butter-milk fingers holding the edges of the book and her long eyelashes glistening like a rainbow in the soft morning sun rays. He can see her long, straight hair falling on her lavender color flowy skirt. He has only twenty minutes to look at those eyes, a canvas of expressions.

He can say whether she is happy, excited, sad, curious, angry or confused by just looking at her doe-eyes. She remains so immersed in reading. Every day. And he reads her page by page journey, through her eyes.

He hears the announcement for the next station piercing his waves of thoughts.

'One day of waiting to see you again,' he thinks while getting down from the train.

After three days...

Ankush shifts in his seat restlessly. His restless eyes are searching for a pair of tranquil ones. She can't be seen anywhere. The train arrives at his station, and he gets down with a heavy heart.

Ankush can't concentrate on his work for the rest of the day. Somehow he feels like she is not okay.

While returning, he visits one of the bookstores. After searching for some time he picks up a book named 'Before I Sleep'. He can only remember this name, the book she had been reading for the last few days.

As soon as he returns home, he starts reading it.

It takes him more than three hours to complete the whole book. He closes it finally, with hollow eyes and a heavier heart. It was completely unexpected.

He spends the rest of the sleepless night praying silently for the first time in his life, to get another opportunity to find her. And this time he just won't let her disappear like that.

But only if he meets her again.

Next morning...

Ankush can't believe his eyes! She is here again, right in front of his eyes! Those pair of eyes...a portrait reflecting her beautiful soul...how he missed those!

Time passes only to keep him looking at her pretty, serene eyes. This time they are looking back at him with surprise and disbelief, he doesn't know why!

He doesn't know how much time has passed. He wakes up from his daydream to reality as she gets up from her seat. He can see her long straight hair from behind her. It's her station! That means he missed his! He just lost the track of time and place!

Without thinking twice, he gets up too and stands behind her to get down with her. He can't help but think of the depressing truth he got to know about her. He guessed that but deep down hoped for it to not be the truth.

Ankush can't wait to talk with her. He can't let her disappear in the crowd. But what will he say?

He gets down with her and starts walking behind the girl maintaining some distance. Still, he can't come up with something to approach her.

Ankush has never felt so awkward in his life before. After 30 minutes of following her cautiously, he is standing here, in front of the main gate of the building- it's a doctor's clinic.

He won't go back without talking to her today. He is determined.

A few minutes pass and then his heart skips a beat as he finds her emerging out from inside.

She looks utterly surprised and unprepared as their eyes meet.

"Hey! I have seen you many times," he starts saying out of the blue. "We…"

"I know!" she cuts him off in the midway as she walks past him without looking at him twice.

"Just a minute! Please listen, I want to…" he says, panicked as she is just about to leave.

-"Want to what?" she stops and asks.

"I really like you…I have come here to talk with you only. I missed my college even!" He keeps saying what he was not supposed to. He feels anxious as she seems to be all eager to get out of his sight. And he just can't let her go like that.

Her expression softens a bit. But in the next moment, her eyes get terrified.

"If you stalk me again, I will call the police," she says angrily.

"Okay…I won't disturb you again," he tries to calm her down desperately. "All I want is fulfil your wishlist being with you," he says looking at her eyes.

He is not in a mood to give up.

"My wishlist?" she stops in the midway. Her eyes are confused.

Ankush takes out the book from his bag,

"I found and bought it…because you were reading it. And…"

"It's about the survival of the cancer patients," she says, tears springing in her eyes. "It's for one of my students."

Ankush gets startled by this sudden revelation. It's not her!

"But why are you so bothered about this?" she asks wiping her tears.

"Because I love you," Ankush blurts out and regrets instantly.

"Is this a joke?" she raises her brows scanning his face.

-No! Why?" Ankush struggles to find some words. "I do!"

"Even after seeing me?!" she seems surprised as she keeps looking at him questioningly.

"Of course! You are so pretty!" Ankush can't understand why she is asking this.

"What?" she points a finger to her lips, "Can't you see this?" She folds her sleeves up, "And this?"

She is looking at him, there is anger in her eyes. But there is some fear too if he hasn't been mistaken.

For the first time, he looks at somewhere else except her eyes. Those are too captivating to look away.

There are white patches around her lips, on both of her hands.

"Can we sit and talk?" Ankush says looking at her. "I don't want to regret for the rest of my life."

"Regret for what?" There is still disbelief in her eyes.

"For not trying." He can see her eyes welling up again.

She fishes out a page of the notebook from her bag and gives it to him.

"What is it?"

"The wishlist." She smiles through her tears, "And you have already signed up to fulfil all of these."

He nods with a smile as he unfolds it and reads the very first line,

Need one man with a pure heart to sacrifice his life.

In that fraction of a second before everything goes black around him, he can see a sinister smile on those pair of eyes, and he can't recognize those anymore.

Black Moon

The clock was ticking slower than the other days- he felt. He was all ready, sitting with his briefcase near his feet and checking his mobile again and again. Finally, the call came at sharp 12 noon. As soon as he got the call, he tied his shoelaces and lifted up his briefcase, ready to go. The woman from the other end gave him the news of her death. Finally. He heaved a sigh of relief, as if the load on his chest, suffocating him for years, was finally gone, for good.

When he reached the hospital, it was hard to say that he had come to visit some dead person. There were no pale faces outside the room, no sound of howling in pain could be heard nearby, no one was seen hugging another one to comfort the fresh pain of losing someone. It was a news as light as the dead leaf blown away by the drooping fall, touching his ears for once and drenching him with a lighter feeling of inner peace, before disappearing into the air. When he was emerging from the room after doing the little formality with a heavy face, there were Tanya and Moon standing near the door. Tanya's face was expressionless, only a bit of concern hanging in there. Moon seemed restless a bit, but was held by her mother, like she was promised something alluring to keep her calm for the time being. George made space for them with a hint of a nod. It was awkward. While talking with the lawyer in the reception, he felt a sharp pain in his left ear. He held the mobile in his right ear but the pain was not gone. It was there the entire time- when they took her body out from the hospital when the three of them got inside the car, and during the entire funeral, it was like the pain was intensifying gradually, and finally, it started diminishing like the dimming flames turning into the leftover ashes through the smokes. While they were returning to their house, Tanya held his hand and pressed it harder than usual, there was no pain or sadness on her face, it was as blank as a white sheet of paper, she stared unblinkingly into his eyes, 'There is no looking back,' she said. 'Despite all the damage she caused to you, she is resting in peace now, but not before giving a slice of that peace to your mind, I believe?' the last question mark sounded feeble like the inside of his head. Moon was sleeping in her lap, her face had a slight hint of a smile which conveyed the comfort she was in. He couldn't remember himself sleeping in peace in his childhood. He gulped like the bitter feeling would be gone by doing so. But his whole mouth and tongue tasted bitter and he felt it spreading through his veins making his blood more toxic than ever. Tanya was watching him while running her fingers through Moon's hair. She was about to say something to him, as her lips trembled a bit, but she swallowed her words. George didn't seem to be fully okay yet. He was not mourning, but he seemed baffled getting this lifelong freedom from the torturous memories. Seeing her alive every day, no matter how faint was her presence, he was being eaten up slowly.

Tanya wanted to tell him to let her be on her own. But George was a responsible man, and he just couldn't let her suffer in her last days, alone. Even her own children abandoned her, but George let her get a good big room at the south-facing corner of their house, and he gave her all the treatment, attention, and care, no matter how superficial they were, he did it all for her, and Tanya was surprised to see his dedication towards his evil stepmother. Let alone taking care of such a woman, Tanya would have abandoned her without a second thought, if she were in George's place. But George was not her, he proved it once again. And every time he did it, she found one more reason to love him harder.

The rest of the day passed in almost awkward silence. They were not missing that woman, she was silent anyway for the last few years, apart from occasionally calling George with her weak voice to turn off the ac or fetch a glass of water in between the duties of the two nurses. Her body was giving up and she just became a mere imprint of what she used to be in her earlier life. She had never tried to interact with Tanya, and to her, she was just like an old piece of furniture occupying a part of their house. And she couldn't wait to get rid of it. She was as silent as a lifeless object most of the time, so Tanya couldn't point out the odds lurking around in the big rooms, behind the curtains, between the gaps of the doors, and beneath the thick dark at the other side of the kitchen window. After putting Moon to sleep, she came to George's room, he was sitting with his back towards the door, his hand on the mouse, clicking on the pictures one after another.

'It feels…' Tanya took a moment to search for the right word, 'Different.'

George didn't respond. His eyes said he was listening to her.

'You know…Moon is very silent, since the time we came back.' Tanya looked at her fingers and then at the screen in front, there was a picture of George with his step-mom and dad, clicked in a studio. Tanya couldn't understand the significance of his reviving those memories. She brought him dinner in silence, as he didn't seem to budge a bit from that revolving chair. She took it as his own process to cope up and let him be. While passing by his room that night, Tanya found him sitting in the same chair and going through the pictures on his laptop. One look and she knew those were the same pictures he was going through earlier that day. She somehow resisted going inside and asking him, 'What the hell are you checking out? That which is gone forever for good and you are reviving your good old memories with her? Have you gone insane? Don't you even have pity? Like, self-pity?' she shouted inside her head and was still not satisfied. George turned around, as he stared at her with his cold eyes as if he was doing some silent calculations in his head. Tanya stared back expecting him to talk. But he was as silent as the suffocating black outside the window, encircling their house, like the death had not only separated their house from the tangibility of the outside world, but also separated each other inside the house. Tanya slept hugging Moon silently, hoping things to get better in the morning.

The next morning passed fast with the daily business-making breakfast, making Moon ready for school, making lunch for George and making his bag ready with his files and laptop for the office. He seemed perfectly normal as he glanced through the newspaper while having breakfast. He kissed her chastely on her cheeks as always, silently saying things were alright between them and in the house. Once he was out for office and Moon for her school, Tanya entered the empty room, there was no trace of an ailing woman spending years. She was sent to the hospital a couple of weeks back, the house was already cleaned, colored, and decorated to make a new playroom for Moon. None of them expected her back. She was in her 80s and the repulsion from the house even catalyzed her death further, what Tanya could conclude. Moon was silent even in the morning. She had always been more on the silent side, but in a cheerful way, staying in her own world. She hoped for things to get fine soon, as it was not worth it, they didn't lose anything at all. Tanya finished her work by afternoon and took bath. Then she made dinner for George. Moon had her weekly dance and guitar classes and she usually spent the day playing with Nina, in Cathy's house. So the house would be for her and George only and she wanted to make some arrangements, more like a small celebration for being free from the shadow of the lady. She dried her hair and made long beach curls with her straightener, slipping into her sea-green silk gown with a side slit till knee, she checked herself in the mirror. If not mistaken, she could find the lost glow in her skin, and her eyes as sparkly as the stars in the still streams of the river. She was back in her school days when she used to get dolled up for sneaking out with George to their movie dates…she can remember their intense make out near the ending of the movies. Most of the days they used to end up being in her bedroom. Tanya used to stay all on her own in a flat shared with two other girls and George used to stay with his evil stepmom while his dad travelled the world for his navy job. She heard her classmates saying terrible things about his mom which would often disturb her, he was her boyfriend after all. But one fateful afternoon she became the main head behind such sayings. It started from describing how she threw her coffee mug to her face to how everyone she slept with ended up committing suicide or destined to a more horrible death. Tanya didn't care about how true were those, as long as those were bad enough to defame her. But she was a real witch and it took her a few hours to get that straight into her head. The calling bell rang when she was rolling the shiny peach lip gloss on her lower lip, curled conveniently. It was just 7:30 and George would not be home until it was 9. She kept her eye on the keyhole and found the delivery boy standing with a bouquet of white and red flowers. She opened the door, surprised. No name, no message, nothing- just a bunch of flowers. The delivery guy left already! *'Gotta be George!'* she thought. Tanya played an indie-pop in the music player and lit some more candles of white and pink color, she lined them up on the dinner table. The light spring breeze was filling up the room occasionally, the candles were kept safe away from the touch of the blowing wind. The lace curtains were flowing away uncovering more dark outside. The food, weather, and the occasion all seemed to fit each other perfectly, it was worth the celebration. She heard a faint sound from Moon's new playroom. As she opened the door a lizard fell on her feet. She was almost about to shout but checked herself. The lizard ran away by that time. She waited endlessly at the dinner table for George. When the clock struck 10, she received a message from George's number, *'I will be late today. Don't wait for me. I am busy.'* The message seemed unusual to her. She called his number and a female voice picked up. Her voice sounded drunk. And she just couldn't understand what was she saying. She cut the call and called his number again. 'Fuck off!' the same female voice shouted before cutting the call. She felt like breaking everything and slashing the throat of that bitch, but she kept her calm as those were not feasible options for her. Not at that moment. Something was unusual and odd about what just happened, she felt. Someone was playing pranks to crack their relationship. One problem solved & another started! Tanya sat quietly for long, and then finished all the food one by one. When she washed down the desserts with a glass of water, the clock struck 11 and there was no trace of George yet. She changed into her nightdress and went to her bed, she tried to stay as calm as possible, and yet she could sense the calmness and darkness just before the storm. The kind of darkness which lets you know that the darker is waiting for you.

At midnight, she woke up with a jolt and found a big black cat licking her feet; there were a lot of pigeons flying circling her house and it felt like they were there to give some news- good or bad she didn't know. The cat stopped licking her feet for a while and sat still. It was Lili, which she threw from the terrace. Or, did she? Tanya couldn't care less about double-checking the facts deeply rooted inside her head. She tried to get up but her hands and legs seemed to be carved inside the bed, and there were only her eyes which she could move. And she kept moving those until she gained back life in her body parts and woke up. George hadn't return yet and the whole house was soaked in the darkness, it seemed like the entire atmosphere was mourning for the bygone. That witch had sucked up even the last bit of happiness, she thought. The house seemed like a part of cemetery, silent and still beneath the flow of time with no sign of seeing the morning again. She tiptoed to the new playroom of Moon, and the door was already opened, the air felt heavy inside, and there was no fresh fragrance of the wall paint as she was getting even in the morning. It was like the grief and guilt buried inside those walls were coming into lives. The empty boxes of the drugs were laying on the bed, and as she touched those, she could feel the touch of warm wrinkled and shaking fingers holding those before swallowing into the stomach, and then…those were mixing up through her old veins to intoxicate her toxic blue blood, one more day…one more drug…and one more splash of forbidden blue in her veins…the same hatred planted inside her when she licked up the salty taste on her lower lip after being hit by a half-empty coffee mug, was now spreading its roots in her loud heartbeats. It was like some foreign objects announcing war against her lucid body. Tanya came out of the room, as she started climbing the stairs carrying the pin-drop silence on her toes, she was in a trance and couldn't recognize the harsh female voice on the phone was the same she loathed for years, she didn't even wonder how those drug packets came to the room after those were burnt and gone? Is there something called 'gone' forever? Is it possible for a life to disappear into nothingness just like that?

As she kept climbing the stairs one after another, like riding in an endless maze, she heard the painful scream of the stars that died light years ago. She was just trying to destroy the dead which never existed, the gap between her and George grew with her roots and branches. His evil stepmother was just a way to divert her attention from the hollowness. To fill her up, she must empty herself fully, as the tip of her feet touched the stone-cold railing, George changed side from a bad dream, he didn't extend his hand to wrap around her, instead he silently dreamt of the red hot marks on his shoulder, behind his ears gifted by his stepmother, which was burning even more with the cold rough touch of the woman lying beside him, with her eyes shining like winning a game.

Tanya remembered the smiling evil eyes on the day the last pale yellow bottle was emptied, she won the battle by starting new with a new body. Tanya felt as light as a feather as her feet left the cold metal railing in their 20th-floor balcony, her eyes closed dreaming of her own evil eyes…the Moon turned black as the house slipped into nothingness for another decade.

The Silence

Silence can be more tormenting than a high-pitched scream at times. It's like soaking in its comfort at first and then being dragged by its infinite depth, where silence is not peaceful anymore, but it tortures you with its hollowness. Bivya was standing still, keeping her nose at a point of the metal patterns, through which she could watch the soundless night. She tried to feel the warmth of the bonfire and the sound of the guitar far away but it was pin-drop silence, so much that she almost forgot how the words feel in the ears or how each letter sounds. It was like a decade since the melodies lost meaning to her. It was like, all were hollow and mere movements of lips which meant nothing to her silent world. It had been more than 10 years since she lost all her hearing abilities in an accident. It was denial at first, but then it was acceptance and rising from the ashes of despair. But for the last couple of years, her body stopped feeling like her own, it felt strange. Like the accident transported her to an extremely silent world that was not ready to accept her. It had been a couple of years since she broke up with Rehan, her 12 years long relationship, which grew as a part of her own, never left her side through thick and thin…all of a sudden it started feeling like some foreign object poking inside her body and there was no relief until she got rid of it. She shifted to her new apartment near her aunt's place in Surat. She didn't have any problem with her job as anyhow she was doing work from home. She wanted some distance and to see how it goes with herself. But since the time she was all alone in the apartment with barely visiting her aunt staying nearby, it was like she could feel the big nest of silence curled up inside her, it was making her whole body some kind of unknown to herself. And all she was feeling was some strange repulsion from herself. Bivya came back inside and tried to concentrate on her work. She was working as a data analyst with one of the MNCs. The office hours were about to get over and she was about to shut down her laptop when a message popped up in her team. The name showed 'S.New'

'Hey! How are you doing?'

'I am good. What about you?'

Bivya typed back waiting for a reply. It was her office application and ID, though her office timing was already over. Bivya waited for a while and then shut down her laptop. When it was midnight, Bivya received a message on her mobile- *The silence you are trying to escape, is a part of you. You can't escape it. It's in your genes…you may not know. You are the first one to carry it in your genes. It will eat you up one day.'* She messaged back - *Who is this?'* But it was not delivered. She installed TrueCaller instantly and her heart jumped in shock as she saw the name- Bivya Mukherjee. But, when did she even have that number or message herself?! She called back, but it was switched off. The cold breeze from outside was blowing away the curtains, as she took a look at the nightscape beneath the moon-drenched sky, at the city sleeping its deepest sleep in eternity, she felt the silence reaching up to her spine, she felt like some specimen with only the existence of a heart inside, which was as soundless as her world was. Bivya approached the balcony with the frozen thoughts of the unheard and unknown she had been hearing since the time she existed. She was sure of getting insane, but then that fateful accident took away her curse from herself. And it took her 10 years to know that curse was still inside her, carried through her silent thoughts, the frozen sound of her bloodstreams, and her eyes making up for the shortcomings of her deaf ears. She felt herself heavy inside, like a pain stuck deep in her throat, suffocating for its voice. Bivya sat there until morning…until the unsettling thoughts subsided in her, but she could feel them alive in her, waiting for some good time to get explored. The whole day passed quickly with her office work and she also had a talk with her mom after decades. When it was nearly afternoon, the maid from the other house rang her bell. Bivya was sipping coffee while wrapping up her work. The urgency on her face was clear and when she rushed over there, her aunt was sitting still in her easy chair, there was still the book held in her hands, her eyes were closed and a slice of soft afternoon sunlight kept her wrapped with its traces on her woollen cardigan, she was not breathing, and she was so cold that it reminded her of the cold storm which passes by her often. Bivya stood there until the crowd gathered there was all gone, and her aunt or the remaining of her aunt left the house forever. The book was still laying on the chair, someone kept it there before taking her, the title read 'No Escape- Beneath the Silence.' Bivya left the place hurriedly, she took her laptop, purse, and a few other things in her backpack and took a cab. She was going back to her house.

Before one week

There was that thing that happened with her again after a decade. She was having sleep paralysis with the vivid hallucination of dying in her easy chair. It felt so real that she sensed death choking her slowly while the dazzling winter was spreading its wings outside. Nature felt so cruel and she watched herself getting lifeless in her own easy chair while feeling its touch at her hands and elbows. It took her longer than usual to get back to her senses, and the world was put on a standstill and it woke up from mourning the moment she could open her eyelids. She watched her niece Bivya walking towards her front door, wearing a nonchalant expression on her face. But her eyes were moving continuously. Like they were trying to find out what just happened. While talking with her over tea that day, she felt her eyes seeing through her- all her nightmares, insecurities, and fear- Bivya was sipping with her tea, her eyes were on the handles of her easy chair, where she kept her hands. She remembered how she was choking in her dream to death while her hands laying still over the handles. She shifted a bit on the easy chair, just then a crow left the branch of a tree to disappear in the grey far away. She felt a déjà vu and it was almost instant to find the resemblance with the vivid dream. Bivya was just about to leave and though she didn't speak anything, she could feel what she was trying to convey. And at that moment it didn't feel wrong but it felt as if the murky afternoon, almost black and white sky outside and the breathless weather- all were conspiring and it was completely fair to happen in real what she just saw. It was terrifying. She closed the door as soon as Bivya left. Bivya looked back at her through the window, but her eyes didn't meet hers. And soon she left her premises. She wished she never came again, as that stale and terrifying feeling stayed with her till midnight until sleep took over her. Since that day there was no direct interaction between them. She could still hear the thoughts of her deaf niece, it said what she saw was her destiny and soon she would meet it. She thought of visiting a doctor once, though she didn't have any such health problems. She even saved the date in her calendar. But when that reminder rang, only the empty walls in her room heard it. Death is terrifying.

The present

Bivya was surprised when she found her own duplicate id and number from where she texted herself. Strange, because she couldn't remember creating those…how could she threaten herself with her own darkest thoughts or fear. She tried to get over the weird feeling as she looked through the sharp cold piercing her face. Her face told there was urgency and so she was on her way to the airport at 3:00 in the night. She could see nothing but the cab sliding into the pitch dark to darker and she felt the silence growing…until it could speak to her ears. All the whispers were nothing but a cacophony of her imaginations since her accident. And once it started to bring brutal meaning, she left her place. But what she feared was inside her. It only grew with the silence around her.

'You have reached ma'am!' the cab driver told her several times, but she couldn't hear. She noticed the airport entrance once she dragged herself out of the thoughts. Sometimes she didn't understand why was she incapable of hearing what's in real and could hear what didn't exist.

While waiting to board her flight, she dropped a text to Rehan, *Meet me in our café, today afternoon. It's urgent.'* It was the same café they took all their decisions in. She had already bid him goodbye once, but this time it was her duty to bid a final one.

The House with a Dream-catcher

1

Dreams are often beautiful and terrifying at the same time. The dreams you see and try to find in your reality but can't find, the dreams with bitter truths you hate to admit, and the dreams which scare you to death and then you remember the feasibility of it happening in the reality.

Simran was waiting for the last one hour in the reception watching every object her eyes could see, starting from the paperweight on the reception desk to the disappeared wings of the rotating white ceiling fan. And yet her turn had not come. Her name was at 5th on the list and she expected it to be quicker as she couldn't be there for long. While she was observing the white papers held between the sleek fingers of the receptionist, someone called her name- twice. The first time she missed it as she was immersed in thinking how she couldn't wait more than five minutes anymore. Next time her name was called and she stood up, 'It's me!' she found a few pairs of eyes on her after noticing her existence for the first time. She had always been like that, disappeared into the thin air, even after being there.

'Hi,' Simran sat on the chair with her hands clasped on the table, 'I want it to be as brief as possible. I have very little time.'

'Sure! As you want!' the middle-aged woman on the other side of the table answered calmly. Every day she used to see such patients, even more, anxious and tougher ones than her.

'First of all, myself Simran.'

The woman nodded, she was already staring at the filled up form in front of her.

'I am facing some problems, though I don't have any such history of mental disorder. Somehow I am convinced that what I am feeling and seeing is real. But…that's what a person with mental disorder feels too, no?'

The woman nodded, though Simran didn't stop to hear her answer. 'I am saying as briefly as I can. My friend, Jasmine…her partner, I mean her boyfriend died one week back, his name is Rakesh and he was your patient, I know…he was doing his counselling to you.'

The woman shifted a bit in her place, but the smile was pasted on her face, she remained as calm as she was from the beginning.

'Rakesh was fond of me since college, everyone knew. But we never had anything between us, he tried to…but I never accepted him,' she paused a bit as the woman in front of her seemed interested, she had her eyes on her, and her face expressed curiosity more than the calmness. She didn't speak though.

'In the final year of our college, he got involved with Jasmine. But his eyes were always on me. Last I met him at Jasmine's birthday party, he even tried to come close and wanted to drop me home. Since that day I never hung out with them. Rakesh was found dead in his room before a week, and since that very day he comes to me…every day…'

Dr. Mithila adjusted her specs as she kept a straight face to let her continue. The girl in front of her was in her twenties, her hair was tied in a neat ponytail, and she would occasionally play with the sleeves of her white color oversized sweatshirt while talking. Her face was round and small, her eyes looked puffy like she slept for long in a stretch. She was biting her pale lips while talking. It was important for her to notice the body language of a patient. Sometimes it gives more than what they talk about.

'He comes with his eyes searching for something. And every time, before he goes back, he stares at me with his blood-shot eyes, those eyes can swallow me up, I think, but I don't know whether thankfully or not, I wake up every time at the same point of time.'

Dr. Mithila's expression said 'I already knew what was coming. Tell me more…'

Simran spoke again, 'Bad dreams, nightmares, hallucinations…these are common, no? But let me tell you, what's happening with me doesn't fall in any of those categories. Every time he leaves a mark. He tries to hurt me in my dream, last time it was a knife, before that it was a lighter…once he tried to choke me with his hands…the marks are still there,' Simran removed the collar of the sweatshirt at one side- there was a round dark red patch of getting choked.

Dr. Mithila leaned forward to have a look, and then nodded like, just for the sake of nodding, 'Do you have those things with you…of Rakesh, I mean the proof as you told?'

'Yes,' she took out a few things and put them on the table, then watched the time on her wristwatch, 'The most important thing. By 5 p.m. sharp, I need to leave.'

'Why so?' Dr. Mithila asked while observing the things kept on the table, her voice was as soothing as the dark cold sea in the midnight. There was a knife, lighter, rope, and a few hair strands.

'Someone I know will come to you for consultation. I want to keep it a secret and don't want to be tagged as a mental,' Simran answered.

'Strange!' Dr. Mithila muttered under her breath, 'What are these?' she picked up one hair strand of around 1 inch in front of her.

'This is of Rakesh. The last time he tried to strangle me, I resisted and his hair was in my fist. After waking up it was still there.'

The doctor sighed silently, 'Have you slept for long? Have you been taking sleeping pills recently?'

'Yea,' Simran looked at her nails kept on the smooth white table. 'But only last day. I thought, if I sleep deep, it may help. But guess what? He won't stop coming. He was angrier last time, for not accepting him. He told that there are people behind his death. And by other people he meant me, I think.' Simran looked at her watch hastily, '4:50 it is. He will be coming anytime here.'

'You told 5:30? I will take time to talk with you if you don't mind.'

'Of course!' Simran stammered while saying, there were drops of sweat on her forehead, it looked like glitter from far, 'here' she gave her a yellow stick-on note with her number scribbled on it. 'I don't know what will happen to me, but call me when you have time. I will need your help.' Simran got up to leave.

'Just one question,' Dr. Mithila asked her calmly, the extra calmness in her voice was to cover up the curiosity, Simran knew.

'Yes?'

'If you are convinced that all that is happening is real, why did you come to a counsellor? Why not any…other one?'

'Maybe for a confirmation,' Simran shrugged. 'I will really need your help…I may. Now I need to go the doctor. Hope we see each other again.'

'One thing Simran, the person who will come and you know him or her, can you say the name? Maybe I can call you on the day he/she doesn't have an appointment?'

'You can check your own schedule…at 5:30. I really can't take the name doc. Thank you,' Simran left instantly without looking back. The things were still on the table, there was no way to understand who did those belong. Dr. Mithila gathered all those inside of a plastic bag as she wondered from where to start. She didn't give away much. Her mobile beeped in the next minute. *Please keep the things safely with you, we may need those soon. Especially, the hair strands…those will help in DNA test.'*

'*Sure,'* she typed back thinking what the hell was she thinking?! A DNA test of a person who was dead and burnt? Another high level lunatic on her list, she smiled unmindfully. She checked her schedule for 5:30, but there was no appointment. The next schedule was for someone named 'Natasha Singh' at 7:00 pm and it had been postponed to the next week. Dr. Mithila thought of updating this to Simran, maybe it was Natasha only she referred to and she was not coming that day at all.

2

Adrija couldn't understand what was going on. Since the time Simran came back, she kept herself locked in the terrace room. She knocked a few times to only hear silence at the other side. She had been behaving strangely since the past week, since the time Jasmine came to their house. They were talking and then Jasmine left teary-eyed. Simran was eight years younger than her. But that was not the reason, she just had never been interested in sharing things with her elder sister. Adrija knocked on the door a few more times, but no one responded. There was a strange heavy feeling lingering in the air of their house. She had been feeling this for a while, something negative in the house. She had never felt such a thing before in her life, she tried to talk with Simran, but she seemed even colder than before. Adrija was about to knock on the door again but she stopped sensing something. The air was filled with something she couldn't recognize, yet felt uncomfortable by its presence. The room inside was silent yet she felt something was going on inside.

The Sun outside was glowing faintly, a bit unusual than the other days, as if she was looking through some sunglasses. She started knocking on the door again…once, twice, thrice…there was no response. She saw Simran entering her room and she was feeling terrified for an unknown reason. She knocked again and then stopped, the sky was half-colored with the black thick clouds out of nowhere and she understood that the door wouldn't be opened from inside. Though she couldn't point out why she wanted to call someone for help, she was alone and stranded in that home, which felt like an island. Adrija shouted while knocking on the door with big thuds, the sound evaporated and then disappeared into the thick air inside the house. She didn't feel like anyone outside could hear it. She held her breath and then entered the kitchen to find something. First, she picked up a knife and rushed towards the closed door, and then she remembered she needed something heavy to break it. Her brain was not working properly as she felt all the negative forces of the universe were collapsing down on her. The door was shut tightly and it would not budge. She rushed to the kitchen again and came in front of the door, where the world seemed to be stopped. After swallowing a deep breath and the darkness spreading outside, she started hitting on the door with all her force, until it fell open inside of her. She didn't even notice the thing with which she broke the door. Despite giving so much energy and making loud thuds, the sound remained trapped inside the home, and the room lay empty in front of her. The crimson curtains were moving lightly with the touch of wind, a glazing spring afternoon stared back at her through the open window. The room seemed to be full of life, so much that it felt unnatural to her.

'Simran?' Adrija called her name while hearing her own breathing getting normal. As she tiptoed inside the room, the coldness wrapped her up, the spring outside remained distant. There was no trace of Simran anywhere near. She opened the wardrobe unmindfully, *'how can one disappear like that?'* she whispered while fidgeting through the clothes, nothing specific in her mind. She opened the showcase next, and a few books fell near her feet. Next, she opened the refrigerator without any specific thoughts and screamed at the very moment.

3

Dr. Mithila tried her number for the second time. It was unreachable. She also dropped a text, but it wasn't delivered. She was getting ready to leave the clinic and then something struck her. She opened her schedule from last month. Most of the slots remained unchanged except for a very few changes like someone got well, or dropped off or...Mithila looked at the name 'Rakesh Menon' with droopy eyes. Suddenly she felt there was less air to breathe inside the room, as the darkness started making her feel nauseous. Her eyes read *'appointment time 5:30 pm'*, which remained empty now. The ticking of the clock suddenly sounded louder than ever in her eardrums, the room felt alive and breathing on her shoulder, there were exactly 5 minutes left to be 5:30 and the clock started ticking even louder with her rapid heartbeats as the room felt like slipped into the snow-age. Mithila ran towards the door while her body started shivering heavily from the inside. The door didn't budge an inch, as she started losing herself with thousand tons of weight pressing on her chest, her eyes remained wide awake into the nothingness, her ears playing a voice from decades ago in a loop.

'Every bad thing happens in my life, I dream of it beforehand, or vice versa…'

'I want you to believe me…I had dreams of dying and then coming to the dream of someone else…it was scary and weird…'

'Your meds are not working. These are bullshit and won't work I guess…because you never believed me from day 1…I am not hallucinating…it's freaking true…' the voice in the air evaporated slowly, as she was immersing herself in the depth of darkness, she could almost hear the silence of her heartbeats while her eyes counting the feathers of the dream-catcher… *'take it! It doesn't work! It can only block the dreams…not the reality!'*

'1, 2, 3…' Mithila started counting the feathers, no…it would be backward counting…she lost track…her lifeless eyes kept staring at the dream-catcher…

4

Adrija jumped back like she stepped on a spring, her hands shivering profusely, her lips trembled to only breathe out dryly…it was at the lowest case of the fridge, Adrija could see Simran laying inside the fridge, eyes closed, in the cold of icy smoke, like she had been sleeping for years. Adrija's brain stopped working and so it didn't question how her 5 feet structure fitted inside that small case of the fridge, neither did it question how could one put herself inside the fridge. She only kept staring back at the face, until it opened its eyes and Adrija was still too shocked to run away…or scream further. Rather she just waited for her to step out. Without knowing Simran's story was ended up like how her dreams wanted it to be, and it was only the dream-catcher…which kept track of all the nightmares…or the future reality.

No Moon Night

Ayesha had been sitting all day by the side of her window. It had been more than three hours since the flight landed. She was ready in her dark red Banarasi silk saree and Kundan jewellery. Her head to toe was wrapped in red and golden saree and jewellery and she looked like a walking jewellery showroom. It was dark and past 5 in the evening when the car stopped in front of their house. She was just about to rush to welcome her elder sister, but then stopped. Whatever she did, it became a problem for the whole family of twenty members. And she decided to never recommend anyone to do arrange marriage. The little artificial love she was getting from her husband was not enough to cover up for all she had to bear. That day was her sister-in-law Dithi's marriage and her whole family was invited. However, her parents couldn't come due to their work, or more than that they were not so much interested to come to a remote place and stay for days without any business- yes, that's what they understood the most- business, calculations, what could come to use of them. Their brains were like programmed machines, by default they could calculate the things which were required and which were not. Ayesha sighed as she checked whether her mangtika was in place or not. She had never worn so much heavy jewellery just like she had never done many things she was doing there which she absolutely hated.

When Ayesha rushed downstairs and hugged Sara, the hall was full of people eyeing them. Sara looked gorgeous in the peach and green lehenga, her eyes were shining like never before, the kind of shine you get only when your soul is truly happy. She decided to spill the beans to Sara on that day itself. She couldn't carry on with the marriage. It was a jail to her, and it was better to break free and stay alone than stay in that jail.

The day passed in a blink and then the much-awaited time came when she was lying beside Sara while looking at the moonlit garden outside. So vast that house was. Was that the only criteria to choose someone for marriage? She looked at Sara who was looking through the window and her eyes still had the shine, she always looked like a free bird as she was. If anything, her marriage only let her blossom even more. She just told Sara about her decision of ending the marriage and after getting over the initial shock and failed attempts to make her understand, Sara almost gave in. The marriage was hers in fact, how could she force her to carry on, if she didn't want to?

'When do you want to tell them?' Sara asked without looking at her, her face was dark because her sister's marriage was breaking, but in reality, it was what Ayesha wanted with all her heart…it was her passport to freedom. It had been hardly a few months and she was young with no kids and burden, life had more she knew.

'As soon as possible!' Ayesha replied promptly. Sara looked at her nodding, 'There is something I need to say. Your in-laws, they arranged something for you, on your birthday.'

'So?' Ayesha asked. 'You want me to delay such a vital decision just for a surprise birthday party?' Ayesha rolled her eyes.

'No, it's more than that,' Sara whispered in her ears, her face and eyes were glimmering in the pale silver shades of the moonlight.

'What is it?' for the first time Ayesha was more curious to know about something else except her decision.

'They are going to gift you one-fourth of this property, on your birthday,' Sara's whisper got lighter, her eyes sparkled like anything, her face looked greedy.

'What the fuck are you talking about? Why would they do that?' Ayesha shrugged, though she silently made a calculation in her head, even one-fourth of this property will be worth crores!

'They…just…' Sara shrugged as she failed to find proper words. 'That's what they said to me, and I was not supposed to say you until it's your birthday!'

'You think this may change my decision of not ending this marriage?' the light rays of moonlight were fading outside and Sara's face looked darker even in the silver lights. 'Not at all! I know you…you are not gonna stay trapped for life. If you think it's a jail, then nothing can keep you here!'

'Then?' Ayesha looked at her elder sister with sceptical eyes. Sara was smiling, she looked as pretty as an angel, but her smile was no less than sinister.

'Is it…?' Ayesha felt the same evil grin spreading on her lips.

'Talk about divorce, once it's yours.' Sara was looking straight through her eyes, and there she could see the heart of her sister beating in as much excitement as she was glowing in.

They paused through a prolonged silence, letting the ecstatic feeling sink in, and then burst into laughing looking at each other as they high fived.

After three months

'What are you saying? You can't delay it forever if you really want it,' Sara almost shouted from the other end.

'I know, but I already agreed!' Ayesha replied looking around her carefully, there was no one.

'Still one week is there, no? But…it's stupid Ayesha! Why would you celebrate Karva Chauth if you are going to get a divorce? God!'

'It all happened so fast!' Ayesha replied as she felt the heaviness of the property and Karva Chauth around her neck. 'They were always together busy in house decoration and planning! I never got a chance!' Ayesha felt suffocated. 'I have decided something just now!'

'What is it?' Sara's disappointed voice came from the other side.

'He will be back from his business trip in the morning that day, I will tell him that day itself, in the terrace. I will not celebrate Karva Chauth, but will tell him about my decision!'

Sara remained quiet for the next few moments. Then she spoke, 'Wow! That's cruel!'

'Is it?'

'Screw it, Ayesha!' Sara took a deep breath on the other side. 'You are not doing charity! I was just joking!'

'Alright!' Ayesha said.

'I have some bank work. Will call you tomorrow. Take care!' Sara said.

'Okay! Bye!'

As Ayesha hung up the call and turned around, her heart almost jumped to her throat, while it started beating faster than anything.

'It's too late! You haven't taken bath yet?!' her mother-in-law asked looking straight into her eyes.

Ayesha did a quick calculation in her head- did she say anything regarding the divorce or pronounced the word during the conversation?! No, thankfully! So, it's manageable!

'Yes, I will just go! I hope you didn't hear my plan to surprise him, on Karva Chauth?' Ayesha made an innocent face as she smiled. *'Shit! What the fuck have you just said?!'* she scolded herself inside.

'Oh! Dear, I heard some parts and guessed it. Don't worry, I am good at keeping secrets.' She smiled. 'You get ready first, your aunts are coming for lunch!'

'Oh! Not my aunts, your lovely sisters…come every other day to spoil my own lunch!' she muttered under her breath while smiling.

'Will wait to see your surprise too, hmm?' she laughed and left.

God! Could it get any worse?!

After 1 week

Ayesha couldn't leave her bed since the morning. Sara called her a few times, but she was groaning with body ache. She was feeling like her body was getting numb from the pain. She gulped down a few painkillers without saying, anyone. But no luck. It was like the whole universe was conspiring against her to not let her accomplish what she wanted.

'Deepak will reach by evening, don't worry dear, I have made juice for you, drink some. You will be fine,' her mother-in-law was standing near her bed. 'What I was thinking is, it can be what happens before getting a viral fever, the season is changing. Mallika and Shila got the same symptoms and it took them one week to get fit…but don't worry, I know all the natural remedies you will need.' She smiled an artificial affectionate smile.

'I don't need your home remedies, can you just shut your mouth! I have things to do today, or it will be too late to get out from this freaking prison!' Ayesha wanted to say, but she sipped her juice silently while nodding to what her mother-in-law said.

'Oh! Moon will come out not before 8:00 pm, and until the Full Moon is visible, you can rest. And good luck with your surprise!' she smiled and left the room while closing the door behind her.

'Sara, what is it?' Ayesha called her number as soon as she saw 13 missed calls from her, she was feeling better though after having the juice.

'Mr. Burman, who was all set to buy your share of the property by this week, is not responding for the last two/three days. He was all set to buy it immediately.'

'What are you saying? You think he may not buy?'

Ayesha had fixed the deal with him at 15 crores for her part of the property, while the whole family went to the temple, she faked illness and Mr. Burman made a visit to finalize the deal. Ayesha was fully ready to sell it tomorrow itself, without giving this family any chance to react or think. But this could hamper her whole plan.

'What if he is busy or something? How can you be so sure?' Ayesha hissed. Sara would go back to Canada with her husband next week and Ayesha already bought tickets to return with them and restart her life, she got her visa too, and Mr. Burman gave his words that he will buy it, he was spellbound by the house and even wanted to have it as soon as possible, how could he become unresponsive now!

'Hey! Are you listening?' there was urgency in Sara's voice.

'Yes, say.'

'There is more!...'

'What?'

'I told the gardener to check on him. As you know, Mr. Burman is Ajay's colleague and the gardener knows both of us as he works for both of us. He called me, like before 10 minutes to say, maybe something is wrong…his house is locked from the inside and he is not replying. He stays alone.'

'What else? Are they are gonna break in or what? Is he dead or something like that?' Ayesha bit her lips. *Just when I think it won't be any more complicated, it keeps taking unexpected turns,*' she thought.

'Sshh! Calm down Ayesha, watch out around yourself. Anyway the property is already yours, divorce will also be a cakewalk. Just keep your calm.'

Sara talked in as composed way as it can be, 'Wait a second! The gardener is calling me! I will call you soon!' Sara disconnected the call, and in the next moment, someone moved away from her door with rapid footsteps. She drew the curtains and found a house full of people busy in their respective works. There were only women and kids in the house, the women were preparing for the Karva Chauth. Men were in their business place, they had family business with factories all over India. Ayesha came back to her room, but before she could call back Sara, her aunts-in-law almost dragged her with them, giggling unnaturally as compared to their age. Only a few women took their lunch that day including her grandmother-in-law who was a widow and two of her aunts-in-law with some physical issues. No one offered her any food or even asked how her health was. But she was feeling good and her body ache was gone completely. It was 3 pm as conveyed by the big pendulum clock in their drawing room, and just 5 more hours to say it to her beloved husband…5 more hours to her freedom and a brand new life. Ayesha noticed her mother-in-law and her two other sisters looking at her from far, on the second floor, while smiling and telling something among themselves. Most probably, they were talking about her and their stare seemed as if they could read her mind.

6 pm, on the day of Karva Chauth

Ayesha looked at her bright and pink face in the mirror, she didn't want to get so much dressed up, but keep it simple, or else it would be unfair to Deepak, she thought. But the women in the house didn't spare her from being decked up like a newly married…but she was so…wasn't she? She smiled looking at herself in the mirror, she was looking stunning in red and golden saree, the jewellery she was wearing for that evening was worth crores, only a few were of her mom, rest all were given by her in-laws. She didn't want any of those though, those didn't make up for her imprisoned life, neither can those be the compensation for her dull, workaholic, fat husband. She was sorry to use such adjectives, but that was the only truth. Simply she was brainwashed to do this marriage. The whole house was chattering, the rooms full of enthusiasm, like someone won some trophy unexpectedly. Behind their too-friendly smiles and behavior, there were darker sides full of greed, unkindness, inhumanity, and she hated it. Ayesha checked her mobile, there was only one missed call from Sara and one text message, she guessed the problem was resolved, but her mood dropped as soon as she opened the message, *'Mr. Burman is dead. Call me once you tell Deepak about the divorce. I don't have a good feeling.'*

'Ayesha, one hour left, you are coming na?'

'Of course…just talking with sis…' she replied without checking who it was.

She called Sara, but the call remained unanswered. She called her repeatedly until it said switched off. Her heart was beating faster than ever in her ears, and she felt alone in the house full of so many people. There was another unread text- it was from Deepak and she was the least interested in checking it.

'Come soon Ayesha! All are waiting!'

'Yes coming!' Ayesha turned around to hear the sound of anklets fading in the stairways. The house felt dipped in silence, the sound of the big clock ticking in the empty hall was echoing in the darkness of the walls. Surprisingly she couldn't hear any sound but her own breathing only in the pin-drop silence. Her mobile rang in the next moment, breaking the freezing silence. It was Deepak, she cut the call in irritation. She tiptoed a few stairs up to check what was going on, there was no sound at all. She guessed that the women were counting time to celebrate once the men of the house arrived. Did all men of the house decide to take entry at 8 too? That was ridiculous, she thought. Suddenly she started feeling cold as her mind kept hovering around what Sara told her. She didn't want to be trapped. The silence in the house felt like growing louder, so much that she decided to go to the terrace. It was 7 pm and her heart was pounding louder than ever. She wished Sara was with her! Not only she wasn't with her, but she was going back abroad within a few days, she was feeling alone and vulnerable. Somewhere nearby a sound of a whistle came floating through the thick air, the weather inside felt unnaturally hot to her,

'It's a bird.' A warm breath touched her shoulder out of nowhere.

'Hmm?' She was so unmindful that she didn't notice when one of her aunts-in-law came to stand behind her. She was wearing a way too bright red saree and jewellery for her age. Her smile couldn't hide her cracked, red, artificial lips. Ayesha couldn't pinpoint the strange odd parts in her or in the whole house, but it suffocated her from day one.

'Only half an hour. You are not supposed to stay anywhere else except the terrace, or, the men of the house will find you before the Moon comes out.'

Ayesha watched her talking animatedly, jaw-dropped *'what the fuck does she mean?'* she wondered, but guessed it must be one of the unsolved puzzles which irked her in this house.

'And that won't be good, you know.' Her aunt-in-law was looking straight in her eyes, but it didn't seem like she could see anything at all, like her eyes were looking through some blindfold. Ayesha felt goosebumps in her hands as if she was getting pushed deep inside an infinite cave. The whole house was drenched in silence, she could feel the women talking but they were too light for being words, only escaping their mouths to evaporate in thin air. Ayesha started climbing the stairs, as the time had come. She tried to keep her calm, as she needed to say Deepak that day, anyhow.

'You are not leaving any soon…are you? This night will be long.'

'And you don't leave when you are one of us,' a lot of whispers, mere words were sending the chills down her spine and she couldn't distinguish the voices from each other, she was feeling dizzy and lighter than feather gradually. She checked the time on her mobile- 7:45, 15 minutes left and Deepak was not there yet, in fact, no one was there yet except those intolerable women.

How could all the men arrive at the exact same time when the Moon shows up? Or, were they getting decked up too, somewhere else and waiting to arrive at sharp 8:00? 'Unbelievable!' she muttered under her breath, in the next moment a WhatsApp message popped up on her mobile. It was from Sara- *'Ayesha, you need to leave the house asap, forget property and money, you save your life first. You are the only living thing in that palace Ayesha, and the women in that house are dead and cursed. The darkness reached till me…I doubt that I can make it…but you must and then come to our house…where our parents are. You escape anyhow, you live…remember.'* She was shocked and baffled, but before she could read the message again, someone swiftly snatched it from her hand, the faces were blurred out, but the scratch of a nail or something sharper stayed with her. The haze was getting darker and the clouds thicker. The time felt still, cold, and halted for eternity. The footsteps were getting louder in her ears, and yet the silence seemed unbearable, as her back touched the railing, the uncountable unrecognizable faces stared back at her face with the pairs of deadly eyes like she was in a nightmare. Ayesha looked up to find the moonlight hidden behind the thick clouds floating around. 'With the curse of this house, we give the same to your blood, you are one of us, and you stay up to see the No Moon night,' the whispers wrapped her up like a cold dead snake suddenly awakened after thousand years of sleep. She read or heard the same lines somewhere or everything just seemed twisted that night. Ayesha wanted Deepak to arrive soon, the terrace was too cold and unearthly, the sound of an unknown bird hooting nearby broke the silence into pieces, she felt the grip around her neck pressing her to suffocation, yet all were standing in front of her at a distance, their bodies looked heavy like submerged islands, the dark sky above was spreading itself until the slight hints of Moon were swallowed by the cold black. Ayesha was feeling lighter than a feather, yet the weight on her chest and neck was suffocating her more and more with each passing moment. The mere movements of the blue swollen lips were whispering something she read and heard before, like the pages hidden beneath thousands of decades. *What you see does not exist, what you hear does. We left our beloved bodies with the curse of not saving our husbands when their bus crashed and our Full Moon night turned into a Blood Moon night that day, since then the Moon never rises on the day of Karva Chauth, the night is the darkest at these hours, there is no Moon here ever until you join us to find the beauty of the deadliest silent night of the year. You join, and we become free, and you learn…you don't always need a body to live,'* the whispers stopped with the prolonged silence as she felt as if another snake wrapping her body tightly. Her vision was blurred and her ears burnt with laughter, she turned around and tried to run, but couldn't move even an inch. The silent footsteps were approaching her with unrecognizable faces staring back at her like those were hunting in a forest. The darkness was spreading fast isolating the cursed palace from the world.

'You escape, you live!' the voice came floating like a tiny nightingale in the murderous night, the shallow breathing was touching her for thousand times in a single moment like countless snakes hissing on her face, they were so loud that her eardrums were about to explode. Ayesha never experienced such a horrible surreal thing in her entire life, not even in the wildest nightmare she had ever seen. But this time, it was not a nightmare for sure. One louder voice started ringing in her head- *'You escape, you live.'* Ayesha closed her eyes and pushed herself down from the terrace towards the dense dark beneath, within that fraction of a second, her eyes caught a glimpse of the Full Moon- it turned blood red.

After one month

Sara took her luggage and walked towards her car. Finally, they were going back to their place. Only this time she was feeling lighter and her bank account heavier. She smiled looking at the sliding roads behind her, it went as she planned, and she had been looking forward to this day since the time she got to know about her being the nominee for all the properties and money of Ayesha. Ayesha…she got everything without any hard work since her childhood, even she came to share her own parents and everything which would have been hers only. Just because her fate favored, she came to snatch half of her things instead of being eaten by a dog in the dustbin where she was found. A few pills and money to their maid was all she had to do to make her hallucinate and paranoid, Sara smiled as she read her bank statement again.

20 crores including the property…all hers, and she got rid of the unwanted curse in her life, finally! The thought made her heart jump blithely, as she strolled towards the airport entrance, behind her husband, and she was so engrossed in her thoughts, she didn't feel the warm breathing on her shoulder or couldn't see the blood-red Moon staring at her in the No-Moon sky.

The Painting of Roma D'Souza

1

Sometimes the calmest things give birth to the most terrifying incidents. Like a seed, planted deep beneath the soil, wrapped in the dark, cold, and utter softness, and waiting to bloom into the unpleasant future…sometimes things take their own turn…irrespective of anything you do or pray for.

Roma D'souza, a 28-year-old research scholar, her life revolved around physics and thesis and in the darkroom experimenting with her favorite optics practicals. She grew up in Chennai and shifted to Pondicherry later. While studying there, she fell in love with the beautiful city. She discovered how there was a layer of spring always wafting through the air of the city in all the seasons. She would often take a stroll along the rock beach inhaling the salty breeze and she couldn't point out why it always felt like her physics research papers or maybe something else…which she had in her blood…it was addictive in a weird way. She was having tea in a roadside stall full of locals and tourists. And a boy with handmade posters in his hands approached her for getting her sketch done…she was not a tourist but wanted to see how someone draws her in front of her eyes. Surprisingly, the boy sketched her in less than five minutes…she looked prettier than what she was in real, it was like an enhanced version of herself. She liked it, only except her eyes…it looked dull and dead. But what surprised her more was the boy denied to accept anything in return. She didn't know whether she was the only one to get the painting for free, but there were a few other people holding his creations, a satisfied smile pasted on their faces. She noticed him giving her the carbon copy of the picture, the real one was with him. Maybe he liked to portray her sweet face, she tried to find the reason. That's what we all do, try to find reason for everything…if it's not found, we make it up. Don't we?

A few days later Roma was sitting inside the lab and then Divyam came with a pile of thick books in his hands, he kept those opened on the front table and without looking anywhere else started jotting down on his notepad. He looked ignorant of the whole world except her, or, that's what she felt like. She remembered what he said to her that day, 'Is this your twins? She looks hotter!' pointing to the painting. Roma smiled in return. It had been more than a week and she couldn't blame Divyam for commenting such a thing…she started wishing secretly to look exactly like her painting. Strange it is…but she couldn't get over how gorgeous she looked, even better than how she would look with makeup. She often used to go to the beach to walk, but never saw that painter again. Mostly she would go there alone after her classes or sometimes during the break time…and that day it was post-sunset when she reached the beach. The sky was tinted with pale yellow and it was getting darker. The ambience was slightly different than other days, also she discovered that she never visited the beach after sunset so far…every time she was there…she watched the sunset from the seashore and returned soon after that.

That day felt somehow odd and out of the place, she couldn't point a finger at it though. While coming back to the home, she felt uneasiness and it stayed with her the whole night. At midnight she got up without any reason…and felt an unusual heaviness lingering in the air of her room…like it was not the room she stayed so far. Her flat-mate Keshvi was sleeping in another room. They never got along that well or became friends, they were just flat-mates…splitting up the rent, and electricity bills, cooking on alternate days and exchanging related talks…that's it. She was doing a fashion designing course and was not her type. But that day she felt like waking her up and having any conversation. But she didn't…instead she went to the balcony and stood in silence. The thought coming to her for the last few days started to cloud her mind…and she just couldn't shrug it off. She pulled out her mobile and started searching for the things eating her head up. After one hour of reading countless irrelevant articles, her eyes started burning. She came to her room and threw herself on her bed, drifting away in sleep.

Next morning Keshvi woke her up…for the first time, 'I thought you running late,' she said staring at her, like noticing something unusual.

Roma took a few seconds to adjust herself in the scorching sunrays flooding the room. She could barely remember the dream she was having, but it was somehow linked with the thoughts she was having for the last few days.

'I want to say something if you don't mind,' Keshvi said, waiting for her to respond, her porcelain face was glowing in the morning light, yet her eyes looked dark as if clouded with thoughts.

'What is it?'

Keshvi stopped herself just before saying something, 'It's nothing…I just…' She was clearly trying to make it up for not saying it. 'I have an important class…see you!' She left the room hurriedly.

That day Roma received a call from her landlord, it was a brief and shocking conversation with him. Without giving any proper reason, she was told to leave the apartment in a month, he just told her it was urgent. But, what kind of? She was clueless except knowing it had to do something with Keshvi.

2 weeks before...

Keshvi

She had never been fully comfortable with sharing her space with anyone, especially when it came to such a creepy person...from day one she found odd things about Roma, like her never closing her room, not even when she went to the university. It was like she was inviting everyone to come and look into her life and get clueless and she enjoyed it. The very first day she entered her room was to find a matchbox, if any, as the gaslighter was not working, and Roma already left for university that day. And she found a lot of candles, a bundle of pictures which were numbered at the back, and a lot of other unusual stuff she couldn't name even. Why will a university-going normal girl have such things in her drawer? She thought of searching the rest of her room as well, she was curious. But, then she doubted what if she kept hidden camera somewhere? She left the room taking the matchbox that day.

But more startling things started happening after a few days. And those things went on for the last 7/8 days. She was just going to say Roma about it that day morning, but stopped herself as some thought crossed her mind- she somehow thought it had something to do with Roma herself, she must be behind it, after what she saw in her drawer, she couldn't trust her fully. She went to the owner and explained all except the weirdest part. And he agreed at last.

She highly hoped that Roma wouldn't think it had to do anything with her. After all, she had to stay in the same flat for one more month.

Keshvi didn't have classes today and it was nearly 3:30 in the noon- just a few hours left for Roma to come back. Keshvi was feeling uneasy, what if Roma found out it was her who told the owner regarding her emptying the flat. She didn't know many people here in Pondicherry that she could stay in some other place for one month. She could tell to Ahan, but he was going to trip that day, and also, he was staying with his two other roommates. Keshvi was passing through the passageway while thinking such things, and she found Roma's room wide open, inviting to come and explore and get trapped as it wanted. Keshvi wondered whether there could really be any camera or not.

After half an hour, the doorbell rang, just when she gathered the courage to look through the things in her room. It was Roma standing right in front of her, she looked pretty in the pink kurta and loosely tied up hair...her face was glowing like she had just gone through a makeover. She didn't smile or look at her directly, only shut her door after entering her room silently. Keshvi had no such workload that day and she stayed in her room while trying to shrug off every bit of the thought bothering her. She knocked at her door when it was around 8:30 at night, generally, they did dinner at that time. There was no response, the light inside her room was on though. She again knocked on the door softly and waited for her response. In the next few minutes, she pressed her ear at the door to hear the low volume of some whispers followed by sobs. This time she tried to push the door and it fell open. 'Excuse me?' Roma turned around, her eyelashes seemed like almost touching her pink cheeks and there were some eyelashes, wigs, nail extensions, and many more things scattered on the floor, which she couldn't figure out instantly.

'Sorry! Just got startled! I will do dinner late today…a lot of work,' Roma said in her normal tone as if Keshvi already got the reason for her being busy and didn't need any explanation.

'Ya! Alright!' Keshvi heaved a sigh of relief inside, seeing things normal. Roma looked all decked up and maybe doing something like clicking pictures or making videos…Keshvi already found some safe and feasible explanations for herself. She just wished to stay and work peacefully with her flatmate in the last month.

She noticed all the windows of her room was open though no view of the Auroville Beach was visible from there like the other times. Roma never opened her window after evening, she didn't like darkness, but then again, how much did she know her flatmate? She did dinner in her room while talking with Ahan over a video call. He was in the airport, leaving for the next week.

'You know, I wondered a lot…but I just think I was overthinking somehow,' she said gulping down the fried chicken piece with a sip of beer. She needed to have some that night.

'I told you already. What you told was…'

'Weird…I know'

'Ya…right,' Ahan said softly, he was always extra cautious to not hurt her by his words. Keshvi was somehow over-sensitive at times and he was quite into bluntly speaking out the truth.

'To be honest, I looked up for the things on the internet…and I found a few stuff…' He ran his fingers through his freshly cut hair…something he did whenever he tried to frame his thoughts nicer than it was.

'What did you find?' Keshvi poured herself the rest half of the bottle after finishing the sixth fry. She had the habit of over-eating while talking or watching something, 'But I found nothing!'

'Well, I found through my friend…dark web or stuff like that you know…and I got to know that something like that actually happened.'

'Wait…you are saying that…it is possible?' Keshvi straightened up, at the same moment, the sound of shattering glasses broke the silence in the other room.

'Yes, in 1938, Rosalin Sawyer, she changed in to a completely different person by her looks, thoughts, attitude, everything within 4 and a half months.'

Keshvi swallowed while absorbing his words.

'She got a divorce from her husband and left her daughter, and no one knows where she went till date.'

'But what was the proof that she changed into some other person and both were not different? Or she didn't have plastic surgery?!'

'Well, for that DNA test, and all other was done, and it was proved. Later her daughter admitted her mom not being happy with herself and got involved with some cult stuff…well, these are all I got on the internet…I mean dark web…and you don't need to dig into it…for your good. There is no proof anyway as such…for us to believe…these…could be made up.

Keshvi nodded, 'What about the other one?'

'Other case…oh…it's…' someone tapped his shoulder in the next moment, the boarding already started and Ahan bid goodbye as he joined the end of the queue. The heaviness was coming back to engulf her again. In the last 5/6 days, her world was shaken as she discovered something in her flatmate Roma. She observed a person changing gradually and it was so intense and fast that it terrified her. She tried to talk with someone who knew Roma, but there was none, even the owner who stayed out of the city. At first, she didn't even get what was happening, it was like Roma's skin tone, eyes, hair, and face changed enough for anyone to notice and then it didn't stop and kept changing with more intensity, each day…it was like a visual representation of a screeching sound asking for attention and then growing louder and louder until it gets unbearable for the ears. Keshvi finished the rest of the drink from the bottle as she couldn't help but dig into the thoughts resurfacing inside her again. She again remembered what she had just seen before a few minutes, Roma was doing a lot of makeup it seemed and the way things were scattered in her room, it looked like she was in a hurry. But why so? Was she trying to cover up the changes with make-up? Will a person change too with such drastic changes in looks? Moreover, was it feasible at all? She remembered what Ahan just said to her, she had no idea regarding this dark web stuff, but if she knew she could have hardly resisted digging into it.

'*Can one person change into another?*' she typed on Google again, only to find a bunch of irrelevant articles about what to do if someone's lover or husband changes, and all. She tried Googling in all the possible ways like, '*can anyone's face change completely?*', '*converting into a new person*', etc. etc. But there was no relevant content at all. After half an hour she gave up. She even searched with the name 'Rosaline Sawyer'. But there was no information at all. She started feeling high and a bit dizzy too as the effect of heavy drinking. The whole house seemed silent, and the weather felt suffocating. She looked through her window, the outside world seemed as silent as her room, everything stood still, not even a leaf was moving outside, it looked like a photograph or painting. She was curious to know what was going on in the other room, she was thinking of peeking into the other room, where Roma was. The clock said 1:30. As far as she knew, Roma used to go to sleep early to attend her morning university lectures. Keshvi opened the door of her room and tiptoed till Roma's room, the air was unnaturally thick and she heard some faint weeping sound in the air. The sound was so faint that it took her a few seconds to hear it properly and understand what it was. She thought of knocking on the door and asking whether she was okay but resisted herself. Something was wrong in that room she could say. She stood there still pressing her ear on the door and the weeping sound continued, it was changing its intensity like Roma was weeping while walking inside the room. She pushed the door slightly and it was open already. Her curiosity was peaking as the alcohol was spreading in her blood. She could only see the darkness inside apart from a narrow stream of streetlights drawing patterns on the wall opposite to her. Keshvi tried to adjust her eyes and within the next few moments, she could see the entire room, the sound of weeping couldn't be heard anymore. She was surprised to see there was none inside the room. She was drunk but not so much that she will miss seeing a person inside a room. Keshvi tiptoed inside the room as her heartbeats rose high, there was a big luggage at the centre of the room and the things were all scattered outside of it, the window was wide open and she felt the salty breeze on her face and hair, it smelt different. Where was Roma? She couldn't see her. The window was wide open. Keshvi guessed that she must have gone out, though it felt very strange. She was just about to switch on the lights when the headlights of a car passing by gave her a clear glimpse of the whole room, and Keshvi felt the shockwaves passing through her spine one after another within the nanosecond of time, her heart started beating heavily and she had no strength to move any more. Before losing her senses, she managed to escape the room and drag herself near the basin to puke, she kept pouring cold water on her head and face until her racing heart became a bit more normal than before. That was the moment she felt the fear crippling her…like never before.

Next day…

Roma and Keshvi's apartment was a mess the next day. The apartment was sealed from the outside and Keshvi was being interrogated while the investigating team was puzzled to see the sight inside of the apartment. The news channels broke into weird headlines depicting the incident. Keshvi was dumbfounded and yet to talk properly. What she discovered last night was not only weird and unreal but also a truth that will haunt her forever she knew.

'Send these for forensics immediately while we search thoroughly all the rooms. And give her time, but make her talk,' the officer-in-charge instructed the team as the boxes were being taken for forensics. Keshvi was sitting in her own room and the whole day passed but she didn't talk. It was near the evening when she talked first, 'It was like she was changing her face…like taking off one mask and wearing another…slowly and gradually,' she breathed out. The windows and doors were still open in Roma's room and the team was about to call it a day but not before hearing from her. There was a wind blowing in the room and Keshvi was feeling nervous sitting there all day, her elder sister was on her way to get her.

'The body you found, is not of Roma I believe, it was like an entire shell…she let go of it and she is out there somewhere,' she said placing one word after another, trying to frame her haphazard thoughts. Her speech was being recorded but no one could understand a bit of it. They understood the mental shock she might have but didn't exclude her from the list of suspects in an obvious way. Keshvi couldn't leave the city anytime soon, but she knew Roma was not dead, she was just changed into someone else.

'You mean her soul? Or, spirit?'

Her elder sister was driving the car, the headlights were piercing the dense dark and the whole world felt so aloof itself. It had just been a few minutes since she got inside the car. Her elder sister Sunita travelled so far to take her to her place as her parents were in another state. Even after meeting her elder sister, which was almost after a decade, she couldn't get even a bit of relief. What she experienced was not only indescribable, but it shook her to the core. The outside seemed too cold, the wind was touching her shoulder like snowflakes. She closed the window, the Full Moon looked too bright beyond the dark cold horizon. The outside looked ethereal, like some hidden unknown part of the universe was fetched in front of her.

'It was a complete mess when I went inside Roma's room yesterday night.' Keshvi shivered while uttering the words. For the first time since yesterday, she could frame a sentence normally.

'You last saw her yesterday?' Sunita turned towards her, the slight hint of the night was radiating in her round face, over the years she gained quite a bit of weight, Keshvi remembered how she used to get teased in her childhood by being called 'toothpick.' She looked vibrant and beautiful, for the first time she noticed as she calmed down slowly.

'You okay?' Sunita again turned towards her, concerned.

Keshvi nodded, 'Thanks!' she said looking at her, 'for coming!'

'You don't need to thank me Keshvi! Can you please tell me what exactly happened to Roma? How did she die?'

'She didn't die. She is alive, and that is someone else, who looked like Roma.'

'What do you mean?' Sunita was as clueless as she could be. 'But you saw her today also, right? It was her! Police too confirmed it.'

'Mask,' Keshvi spoke keeping herself as calm as possible, 'Last night I went inside her room…for the last few days I observed something strange, her face was changing gradually and then the change was rapid…like, by every moment she was changing into someone else.' Keshvi looked through the window to find the sliding deserted roads behind their car, she even found a few bats flying over nearby. Sunita looked so intrigued and surprised that she slowed down the car, 'Please carry on.' She put one hand on her shoulder to show her assurance before putting it back on the steering again.

'It was not something ignorable, the change in her face was so loud and unreal, like seeking for attention in a bad way, and then one day, I went through her stuff when she was not in the flat and I found absurd things…candles, books filled with sign languages, it was scary and I was sure she was into something like a cult or black magic stuff, I can't say exactly what as I have very less idea about all these. But that was harmful I knew.' Keshvi stopped for a while to catch her breath.

'Is that what killed her, you mean? All that you saw yesterday night too?" Sunita asked in one breath, her eyes looked curious, naturally. Keshvi knew that Sunita was quite shocked to hear such things from her.

'Yesterday evening when I went to her room, I saw her face got changed…almost totally…and there were eyelashes, nails, wigs, everything scattered inside the room.'

'She was doing make up, right?' Sunita asked, her voice sceptical, her face looked doubtful too. She was like weighing through her words which side to take- to believe, or, to not believe Keshvi? Their car crossed the main road and was sliding through the pitch dark engulfed in the silver of the moonlight, the trees on both sides were making shadows of unreal shapes. The wind didn't feel snow-cold like before as Sunita slid the window up. The night was perfect to give anyone hallucinations and Keshvi also wondered for a while, did she hallucinate all that?

'It was not makeup, it was a different face put on her body, and now I can say I am not sure about how much she changed, maybe it was more than her face!'

'And…what about her body they found yesterday?' Sunita furrowed her brows, in that little hint of light her nose piercing was glistening. She looked confused but too pretty, it was like time made her even more beautiful. Keshvi understood that Sunita was trying to connect all the dots and was impatient to hear more.

'Oh! Wait…are you saying that…she just left her face, body, everything…like…like…' Sunita fumbled for words, 'Changing dress or a shell? And she is out there, somewhere else…in another form?'

Sunita indeed was brilliant, Keshvi thought. She didn't need to find the right words and try hard to make her understand like she had been doing since morning. Keshvi nodded. For the first time in the day, her heartbeat was getting normal. Keshvi didn't know what Sunita thought, but she kept driving with a straight face. Keshvi kept quiet expecting her to start shooting questions soon. As she kept driving through the still silent roads, some unknown fear started crippling Keshvi. She didn't know how much time had passed as she immersed herself in the thoughts of where exactly was Roma? And how was she like now? What if she came to take revenge? In fact, Keshvi was the one to say to the landlord about her doing black magic and all. It started drizzling outside while they were still driving on the highway, the Moon was half-drenched behind the clouds. Sunita was silently driving and occasionally looking at her conveying to keep her calm. She thought of asking Sunita something but then decided to keep silent. After a few minutes, their car stopped in front of a petrol pump.

'Need to fill in…give me a few minutes,' Sunita said as she got down from the car. Keshvi was going to offer her an umbrella, but she was already outside. Keshvi started feeling cold again as the drizzling continued outside. The situation looked ethereal- sitting inside a car with her elder sister after six years on a deserted road, in such an eerie situation. She couldn't wrap her head around what happened to Roma. She looked at her left side to find Sunita approaching the car as she was done, she was limping slightly on her left leg, for the first time she noticed. Keshvi felt a slight shiver through her spine. It was exactly like Roma, the way she was walking. Keshvi was alert on her seat, her gaze piercing Sunita to find any possible clue. There wasn't any. In the next two minutes, Sunita was beside her, driving again. 'I got hurt in my leg a few days back, it really hurts,' she told in a casual tone. Keshvi heaved a sigh of relief. She was just overthinking. Keshvi took a deep breath to calm her down.

2

She was near a rugged cliff, panting for air, her eyes were burning red which stared back at the setting sun spreading too much red in the sky. Keshvi was standing in front of herself and she tried to shout for help, but couldn't. She was getting breathless more and more until Keshvi came and pushed her off the cliff.

Keshvi woke up with a jolt to find Sunita staring at her with her big, round concerned eyes, 'You okay?' It was still midnight and their car was stopped at the side of the highway.

'Yes!' Keshvi didn't feel like herself at all, 'I saw something…I saw myself in front of me…in my dream,' she started panting just like she was doing in the dream she just had. 'I was someone else…I don't know who but it felt familiar and yet I was not Keshvi…I…am not feeling like myself…' her words trailed off as it started raining heavily outside, Sunita looked puzzled yet her face conveyed she believed what all was said.

'There is something wrong,' Sunita swallowed. 'I don't know how it is possible…but…' Sunita slid down the window on the one side of the car to move the rearview mirror. It was splashed with water droplets, Keshvi screamed in the next moment, she didn't fail to recognize Roma staring back at her in the mirror.

About the Author

Ishita Banik is a best-selling Indian author. After completing Masters in Computer Application from the University of Calcutta, she left her M.tech soon after getting admitted and chose the path of her dreams. She has written five novels since 2018 and dreams to live in this world of creativity till the very last day of her life. Apart from writing, she loves travelling, exploring new things, and getting drenched in the beauty of sunrise and starlit nights.

www.ingramcontent.com/pod-product-compliance
Lightning Source LLC
LaVergne TN
LVHW091709190726
843493LV00001B/223